Reader favorite Rhonda Nelson
is back with more....

MEN OUT OF UNIFORM!

These hot Southern heroes have spent years
taking on anything the military could throw
at them and they always came out on top.
So why do they get knocked off course by
the first sexy woman who crosses their path?

Don't miss

THE CLOSER
September 2013

and

THE NATURAL
January 2014

There's nothing like a man in uniform...
or out of it!

Blaze®

Dear Reader,

Fall is getting ready to make its appearance in my little part of the world. The days are getting shorter, the nights cooler and football fever is in the air. (Not that I care, because I don't watch football, but there are a lot of people in my family who do ☺.) I always look forward to this time of year, when Mother Nature says it's time to rest, soup is the meal of choice and the scent of a wood-burning fire surrounds me. It's the perfect time to curl up with a good book—one with a *very* hot hero—and fall into the story. And Griffin Wicklow is certainly hot....

Former Ranger Major Griffin "Griff" Wicklow has left the military for honorable reasons—he's the only match to his half brother, Justin, who needs a kidney transplant and will ultimately die without it. Griff eventually trades his career for Justin's life and the new path he finds himself on leads him directly to Ranger Security. Accustomed to dodging bullets and IEDs, Griff's used to a certain level of tension, but when his first assignment for Ranger Security involves guarding a jewel-encrusted bra—and the hot little liaison who must travel with it from the jeweler's company—the tension Griff's experiencing is of a decidedly different variety. And man, does he like it.

I love to hear from my readers, so please be sure to check out my website—www.readrhondanelson.com, like me on Facebook or follow me on Twitter @RhondaRNelson.

Happy reading!

Rhonda

The Closer

—

Rhonda Nelson

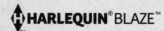

If you purchased this book without a cover you should be aware that this book is stolen property. It was reported as "unsold and destroyed" to the publisher, and neither the author nor the publisher has received any payment for this "stripped book."

Recycling programs
for this product may
not exist in your area.

ISBN-13: 978-0-373-79767-7

THE CLOSER

Copyright © 2013 by Rhonda Nelson

All rights reserved. Except for use in any review, the reproduction or utilization of this work in whole or in part in any form by any electronic, mechanical or other means, now known or hereafter invented, including xerography, photocopying and recording, or in any information storage or retrieval system, is forbidden without the written permission of the publisher, Harlequin Enterprises Limited, 225 Duncan Mill Road, Don Mills, Ontario, Canada M3B 3K9.

This is a work of fiction. Names, characters, places and incidents are either the product of the author's imagination or are used fictitiously, and any resemblance to actual persons, living or dead, business establishments, events or locales is entirely coincidental.

This edition published by arrangement with Harlequin Books S.A.

For questions and comments about the quality of this book, please contact us at CustomerService@Harlequin.com.

® and TM are trademarks of Harlequin Enterprises Limited or its corporate affiliates. Trademarks indicated with ® are registered in the United States Patent and Trademark Office, the Canadian Trade Marks Office and in other countries.

Printed in U.S.A.

www.Harlequin.com

ABOUT THE AUTHOR

A Waldenbooks bestselling author, two-time RITA® Award nominee, *RT Book Reviews* Reviewers' Choice nominee and National Readers' Choice Award winner, Rhonda Nelson writes hot romantic comedy for the Harlequin Blaze line and other Harlequin Books imprints. With more than thirty-five published books to her credit, she's thrilled with her career and enjoys dreaming up her characters and manipulating the worlds they live in. She and her family make their chaotic but happy home in a small town in northern Alabama. She loves to hear from her readers, so be sure to check her out at www.readrhondanelson.com, follow her on Twitter @RhondaRNelson and like her on Facebook.

Books by Rhonda Nelson

HARLEQUIN BLAZE

For an old friend and his beautiful wife
for reminding me what *real* romance is all about.

Prologue

GRIFFIN WICKLOW SAT on the front porch of the house and idly tossed a baseball into a glove, though there was nothing idle about the rage simmering inside him.

Lazy bumblebees buzzed around the hydrangea bush while their dogs—Brooks and Dunn—took shelter beneath its shade in a vain attempt to combat the heat. It was sweltering—he could feel the sweat sliding down his back—but the heat matched his mood, so rather than go inside and cool off, he remained on the porch.

And he watched. Glared. Not that it made any difference.

Every time the door swung open, he could hear his mother, her voice choked with desperation and as much dignity as she had left, plead with his father as he made trek after determined trek to his car, his arms loaded down with his belongings. Griff's little sister, Glory, hadn't quite yet realized what was happening and was peppering both parents with questions. Innocent ones like, "Can I have chocolate milk?" and "Where is Daddy going?"

His lips curled into a bitter smile.

On second thought, that last question wasn't so innocent after all. Gallingly, *everyone* but Glory knew where their father was going. That's why the neighbors had manufactured reasons to be outside, so that they could watch the drama unfold before them firsthand. As if his family's humiliation and pain was for their entertainment.

Across the street, Mrs. Johnson pretended to water her flowers while shooting covert looks across the way. Next door, Mr. Thigpen lingered by his mailbox, appearing to read a circular as he, too, shot furtive looks toward their house.

In and out his father went, over and over again, and with each slam of the screen door, Griff's anger intensified into a white-hot ball of fury, one that made his insides throb, his hands shake and, to his resentful shame, a lump swell in his throat.

After a cursory glance inside the car and trunk, his father closed the lid. He stood there for a moment, his gaze lingering at a spot on the back tire, then he sighed and made his way back to the porch. He didn't go into the house, but rather stopped before Griff.

"I know you don't understand this now, but it's for the best."

Griff looked up and merely smirked at him. "Oh, I think I understand better than you think I do. Your girlfriend is pregnant. You've started a new family and are chucking the old one." He grimaced, continued to toss his ball. "Nothing too difficult to understand about that."

His father's hands fisted at his sides. "It's not that simple. These are adult matters, things you couldn't possibly understand."

The hell he couldn't—Griff knew selfishness when he saw it—but he wouldn't argue. It was pointless and somehow Griff knew his silence was more painful for his father than if he spoke.

"I'll be in touch," his dad said. "I promise. We'll do something for your birthday next week. Go to the batting cages, work on your swing."

A spark of hope flared, but he quickly snuffed it out. They were only words. Maybe even good intentions, but Griff knew better than to believe them, promise or not. He didn't expect his father to show up for his thirteenth birthday any more than he imagined he'd be around for his thirtieth. He might have just now worked his way around to leaving them, but he'd checked out more than a year ago when he'd met *her*. Priscilla. How odd that he could hate someone he'd never met, but he did.

His father took another deep breath, one that seemed to swell enough to sever all ties, heralding the end. "You're the man of the house now, Griff. Look out for your mother and sister." He turned abruptly and made his way to the car, then backed out of the driveway and drove away.

He never looked back.

He didn't send so much as a card for Griff's thirteenth birthday, or any birthday thereafter.

So much for promises.

1

FORMER MAJOR GRIFFIN Wicklow had heard countless tales about Ranger Security and their often bizarre assignments—ensuring the safe passage of fertility statues, finding lost Confederate treasure, recovering Truffles, the dognapped millionaire—but this...

This had to take the top spot for the Strangest Assignment Ever.

He stared at each of the founding members of Ranger Security in turn. Brian Payne, the Specialist, whose cool demeanor and keen attention to detail was legendary. Jamie Flanagan, a proper genius who'd been a notorious player until he met and married Colonel Carl Garrett's granddaughter, and Guy McCann, the Maverick, whose ability to skate the thin edge between recklessness and brilliance was still locker-room lore.

When their expressions didn't change and he was sure that this wasn't some sort of joke, he looked at the photograph once more and struggled to find the appropriate response. One that wouldn't make him appear ungrateful for the job, because nothing could be further from the truth.

He cleared his throat. "I'm escorting a bra from West Virginia to New York and back again?"

"Not just any bra," Payne corrected levelly. He hooked a leg over his knee and leaned farther back into the comfortable leather chair he currently occupied. Downtown Atlanta was framed in the window behind him, glittering with glass and steel. "That's a Rossi creation, designed exclusively for the Clandestine Lingerie Company."

Though Griff had never had any reason to purchase anything from the iconic lingerie company, he could certainly remember thumbing through the catalogs in his teens. His lips twitched. They'd been a source of inspiration, for lack of a better term, and were more easily procured than the traditional skin magazines.

"And that bra, in particular, is worth two and a half million dollars," Jamie Flanagan added. "Naturally, Montwheeler is keen to protect its investment."

A tremor of shock rippled through him. Griff felt his eyes widen and he whistled low. "Two and a half million? For a *bra?*"

Guy shrugged. "It's good advertising for the Montwheeler Diamond Company, for Clandestine Lingerie and the jeweler—in this case, Frank Rossi—who was tapped to create the design. Ultimately, Montwheeler gets the jewels back. They'll put the bra up at auction. If it doesn't sell, they haven't lost anything—they still have the stones, after all, and it's Clandestine who covers the cost of the designer. As far as PR goes, it's brilliant."

He supposed. Still…It was hard to believe that people actually spent this much time and money on something so…unimportant, frivolous even. Given what he'd seen over the past several years in service to Uncle Sam—the death and destruction, the horror, the poverty—it was hard to reconcile this new assignment to those he'd had in the past. He swallowed.

But that's exactly what they were—in the past.

Thanks to some misguided sense of duty and honor—to the very person who'd inadvertently wrecked his family and prematurely propelled him into adulthood, no less—he'd decided a career change was in order. Could he have continued in the military with one kidney? Probably. But given the prep, surgery and post-op care, not to mention his mother's and sister's continued come-home pleas, he'd ultimately decided that Providence was trying to tell him something. Once he was certain of the job at Ranger Security, he'd initiated the necessary paperwork.

And the rest, as they say, was history.

Whether or not this new life was going to be an improvement over the old one remained to be seen. He certainly couldn't find fault with the benefits package, that was for sure. In addition to a very healthy salary and a fully stocked, furnished apartment, a company car had been waiting on him when he'd arrived this morning. He'd been given a laptop, a cell phone, a new Glock with permission to carry concealed and a sincere slap on the back that had welcomed him into the fold.

For whatever reason, that slap had been more appreciated than anything else. He'd instantly liked all three men, felt an immediate kinship. As former rangers themselves, they *got* him. Honor, duty, service. They were more than words; they'd been a way of life. His new employers knew the decision to leave hadn't been made lightly, knew that coming to terms with this career change was a struggle. Because it wasn't just the career—it was a different world, one he knew his place in.

And here? Well, that still remained to be seen.

"We've been hired by Montwheeler to ensure the safety of the bra," Payne continued. "You're to pick it up at Rossi's in Shadow's Gap, West Virginia, at three tomorrow afternoon—a representative of Rossi's will accompany you—and take it to New York, safeguard it throughout the show, then return it to Rossi. Rossi will make any necessary repairs before Montwheeler takes possession once again."

All things considered, it shouldn't be too difficult. He nodded. "All right."

Guy's lips twitched with humor. "There are worse things in life than going to a lingerie show," he added. "Leggy, half-naked models parading about and all. Consider it a perk."

Griff grinned. There was that. He hadn't been with a woman, naked or otherwise, in months. No time. Between deployment, surgery and recovery, he'd had very little opportunity to find comfort in the softer sex. While he'd been recuperating at his mother's, one of Glory's friends had visited frequently and had less than subtly let him know that she was available, but Griff knew the minute he showed the least little bit of interest, his mother and sister would have him married off before he could say "I don't."

In fact, the settle-down-and-find-a-nice-girl refrain had been coming off his mother's lips a little too frequently for comfort, particularly considering he had no plans—immediate or otherwise—to marry. He carried the Wicklow gene, Griff thought darkly, and, based on family history, Wicklows were incapable of being faithful.

It wasn't a theory he was willing to test.

Thankfully, he'd never met a girl who'd made him want to risk it.

Besides, he already had a family to take care of, the one he'd had since he was almost thirteen years old—his mother and sister.

"Do you have any questions?" Payne asked.

Griff shook his head, tuned back in to the present conversation. "None that I can think of at the moment."

"All right, then." Payne stood, signaling the end of the briefing. "I think that about covers it. You know where to find us if you need anything."

Griff and the others found their feet, as well. He shook Payne's outstretched hand. "I don't anticipate any problems."

Payne merely smiled, but didn't comment.

Griff had almost reached the door when a thought struck. He stopped short and turned around. "The Rossi representative? They're aware that I'm in charge, right?" Considering their company had designed the bra, he could see where they might feel a certain ownership. He didn't want to waste precious time and energy on a power struggle.

Something flitted across Payne's face—humor, maybe?—so fast Griff was inclined to believe he'd imagined it. Jamie suddenly developed a keen fascination with the toe of his shoe and McCann turned a small chuckle into a pitiful replica of a cough.

A finger of unease nudged Griff's spine.

"The Rossis are aware that you were hired by Montwheeler and that, as such, you're the ultimate authority on how to protect the piece."

Good, Griff thought, still puzzled over their odd behavior. He was accustomed to giving orders and having them followed without question. That this Rossi person had been made aware of the status quo should make his job easier. He could always pull rank, of course, but it was better if he didn't have to.

Determined to get started, he nodded and made his exit. He'd just walked into reception when Juan Carlos, their office manager, halted him with an urgent *psst*.

Griff frowned and walked over to the thin Latino man's desk. Juan Carlos wore a perpetually longsuffering look and the latest in men's fashion, and sorted his ink pens by color. "Yes?"

Juan Carlos slid a picture across his desk. "Does this woman look familiar?"

Griff picked up the photo and studied it. One look had confirmed that he didn't know who the woman was, but he was curiously struck by her nonetheless. Inexplicably, his stomach tightened and a tingling sensation flitted through his chest. He told himself it was indigestion and batted the curious sensation away.

Long, wavy dark brown hair framed a face that was heart-shaped but lean, emphasizing her high cheekbones and lush mouth. Her skin was luminous, practically glowing with good health and vitality. It looked soft, touchable. Her eyes were large, an unusual misty gray and surrounded by thick, sooty lashes. Hidden humor lurked in that gaze, as though she was privy to some private joke. She was smiling, almost shyly, and there was something about that hint of vulnerability that made her especially attractive. She wasn't merely beautiful or pretty, though those words certainly fit. She was...lovely.

And hot.

Oddly shaken, Griff handed the photo back to the office manager and shook his head. "She doesn't look familiar, sorry."

Juan Carlos swore hotly under his breath. "Damn them. This isn't funny anymore. They can't keep playing the same joke on every new agent. It's not professional."

Joke? What joke? Confused, Griff frowned. "Come again?"

Juan Carlos straightened, then seemed to give himself a little shake. "No worries, Major Wicklow, you'll recognize her soon enough," the little man said grimly. He gathered up a sheaf of papers from his desk, then stood and swiftly retreated before Griff could press him for further clarification.

Rather than dwell on the bizarre exchange, Griff

shook it off. After all, he had a strategy to plan…and a *very* expensive bra to protect.

PAYNE WAITED UNTIL he was certain Griff was out of ear-shot and then turned to face the other two. He arched a questioning brow. "First impressions?"

"I don't think we could have matched him up to a better first assignment," Guy said, dropping back into his chair. "If anyone needs to be able to find the humor in a situation, it's him."

Jamie nodded thoughtfully. "I agree. Granted, he hasn't had a lot to laugh about of late, but by all accounts he's always been rather…serious."

Thanks to Charlie, their female hacker extraordinaire, they knew more about Griff than he'd no doubt be comfortable with. School records showed a well-rounded, bright, promising athlete until the seventh grade. Beyond that, various counselors and teachers had noted a distinct withdrawal from social clubs, sports and the like. By all accounts, Griffin had abandoned normal school-age pursuits and started working various odd jobs. He cut grass, hauled hay, raked leaves, bagged groceries, walked dogs, anything that would net him a cash return for his services. And the impetus that had caused this change?

His father had left.

As the only "man" left in the house, amateur analysis suggested that he'd prematurely stepped up to try to fill his father's role and had developed an early sense of obligation and duty. No doubt that's what had appealed to him about the military, where the lines were clearly

Rhonda Nelson   19

drawn and order was law. He'd earned an ROTC scholarship, graduated at the top of his class and quickly moved onto Ranger School. He'd excelled in the military, had been routinely given difficult assignments because he'd proven time and time again that he could see them through and, as a result, had been given the nickname "the Closer."

A quick glance at his financials had revealed that, in addition to buying the house his mother and sister currently lived in, regular monthly transfers had been deposited into his mother's account. Both his mother and sister had obtained their nursing licenses and worked for a small home-health company in Chapel Crossing, just outside the city. Payne would be willing to bet that Griff had paid for that, as well.

"He seems to have recovered well from the surgery," Guy remarked.

"He does," Payne agreed. "Dr. Jackson cleared him for work without any restrictions, so I think the physical toll is past him." In addition to Griff's own doctor, Payne had insisted that theirs take a look at him, as well. Better safe than sorry, right?

Jamie shot him a look. "What about his emotional health? You think his head is on straight?"

Payne hesitated. "I think it's on straight enough to do the job. I think he's struggling with the sudden, unwanted relationship with his half brother."

Guy grunted knowingly and his eyes widened. "That had to have raked up some shit. Go seventeen years without hearing a peep from his father and then a phone call out of the blue from the man, asking him to give up a kidney for the son he actually raised?" He grimaced significantly. "That would screw with any guy's head."

"Yeah, but it wasn't the kid's fault, was it?" Jamie added. "Griff's dad was the bastard, not the boy."

"And the kid was dying," Guy said. "It wasn't like Griff had a choice."

True enough, Payne supposed, but it couldn't have made the ordeal any less difficult.

And no doubt figuring out where to go from here was going to take serious thought and consideration. Even from the outside looking in, the family dynamics were a nightmare. Even if Griff decided that he wanted to get to know his little brother, how would his mother and sister feel about it? Would they approve? Or would it be too painful for them? He didn't envy Griff, that was for damn sure.

"Are we certain Jessalyn Rossi is going with him?" Jamie asked.

"Last I heard," Payne told him. "She wasn't thrilled with the idea, but I gather her father is a bit of a recluse and her siblings no longer have anything to do with the family business. It's her or no one and, evidently, letting someone else accompany the bra isn't an option either."

"What do we know about her?"

Payne chuckled. "She's hell on wheels. Literally. She works for the company and by all accounts is a top-notch jeweler." He hesitated. "In addition to that job, she moonlights as a mechanic and dabbles in amateur stock-car racing. She's doing quite well this season," he added mildly.

Both Guy and Jamie swiveled to look at him, their faces identical masks of shock.

"Seriously?" they echoed.

Payne nodded, enjoying their expressions.

"Well, that should certainly make things…interesting," Guy remarked.

"Something needs to," Jamie remarked, tossing a jelly bean into his mouth. "This case seems pretty cut-and-dried." He shot them a sardonic smile. "In other words, boring."

Payne smiled but wasn't convinced. He had an odd feeling about this assignment—a premonition of… something he couldn't seem to shake—and intuition told him there was more to this mission than met the eye.

He just hoped Griffin Wicklow was ready for it.

2

JESSALYN ROSSI WIPED her hands, stuffed a grease rag into the pocket of her coveralls, then dropped the hood into place with a soft click. She turned to the car's anxious owner. "It's the water pump, Walter," she told the older man. "You know I'd fix it for you if I had time, but I've got to go to New York for a few days for Dad." A shudder of dread rippled through her middle.

Hell would undoubtedly be a more pleasant destination.

She didn't mind the city, per se, but spending any length of time around stick-thin, surgically enhanced lingerie models wasn't her idea of fun. She had enough body-image issues, thank you very much. She didn't need to compound them by being made to feel like a gluttonous hog with a sugar dependency. If it had been up to her, she and her "child-bearing hips," as one kind but misguided soul had once told her, would stay here.

Unfortunately, it wasn't up to her.

Walter's frown deepened, but he nodded nonetheless. A senior citizen on a fixed income, she was sure the older gentleman would have preferred that she fix his car because he knew she'd be willing to take a basket of garden vegetables in exchange for parts and labor.

"Take it to Shorty Greene and tell him I sent you." She grinned at him. "I know for a fact that the deer got into his tomatoes and he's running short." And she would call Shorty and promise to make up the difference. So what if he chided her for being such a soft touch, telling her that the rest of the full-time mechanics in Shadow's Gap would thank her not to accept produce in lieu of cash. It was a refrain she'd heard often enough before from her old mentor.

Shorty Greene, one of her father's oldest friends, had taught her everything she knew about cars. While nothing gave her as much pleasure as her jewelry, casting the perfect set and embellishing it with beautiful things, being able to rebuild a motor came pretty damn close. Having spent every summer from the time she was six to sixteen with Shorty and his late wife, Sybil, while her parents were at various trade and gem shows, Jess had found she liked being in the garage with Shorty more than being in the kitchen with Sybil. She preferred the smell of motor oil to cooking oil and liked the weight of a tool in her hand.

It had all started innocently enough, by her merely handing Shorty the appropriate tools, but it hadn't taken long until she'd wanted to know how the tools worked. Figuring out why a car wouldn't run properly quickly became a mystery she had to solve and once she'd solved it, she reveled in fixing it, setting things right. Listening to a motor catch with the first turn of the ignition, then hearing the engine purr. She smiled, remembering.

Music to her ears.

Naturally, her mother, who'd sadly lost her battle with cancer when Jess was seventeen, hadn't approved of a teenage daughter with grease under her nails. But she'd later revealed that she admired the fact that Jess hadn't let her gender get in the way of doing something she loved. After all, it was one thing to tell a kid they could do whatever they wanted and then discourage them when they chose something not deemed "proper."

This was the argument Jess had used when she'd wanted to start racing, as well. Not surprisingly, it had come in very handy.

Walter was too proud to look relieved for more than half a second, but his shoulders relaxed and a smile broke across his weathered, lined face. "Well, you know I've got plenty of tomatoes," he told her.

She inwardly snorted. He had plenty of everything. His green thumb was positively legendary in Shadow's Gap. "I'll give Shorty a ring and let him know you're coming. You don't want to drive any farther than his place, though, Walter," she warned. "If the car over-heats too much, you'll crack a head and then you'll really be in trouble."

"I'll go on over there now," he said. "Thanks, Jess." His brow wrinkled once more and he shot her a look. "You're going to New York?" he said. "Today?"

Jessalyn's cheeks puffed as she exhaled noisily. "Unfortunately, yes."

"Will you be back in time for the race on Saturday?"

No, dammit. She'd still be babysitting the bra. "I'm afraid not."

He grunted, his face falling into a moue of regret. "That's a shame. I think you could have given Lane Johnson another run for his money."

She did, too. Lane Johnson was a cocky, loud-mouthed blowhard with more luck than skill and a sickening following of track whores—not to be confused with crack whores, though they could be easily mistaken for those as well—who stroked his giant ego, among other things, Jess thought with a shiver of disgust. They contributed to his misguided perception that he was, first, God's gift to women, and second, almost on par with Dale Earnhardt Jr. behind the wheel.

He was neither.

Gallingly, while she'd taken plenty of heat for being a "woman driver" when she'd first started racing, she'd quickly won the respect of the majority of her fellow drivers. There were always going to be a few with the old-school boys' club mentality—she'd be foolish to think otherwise—but of them, Lane was definitely the loudest. She'd thought beating him would shut him up, but instead he'd upped the trash talking and told everyone that he was going to "put her in her place" the next time they shared asphalt.

That should have been this weekend, but she hadn't been able to get either of her siblings to accompany the damn bra, so now it was going to look as though he'd scared her away.

As if.

It made her blood boil.

Jess had always been proud of her Rossi heritage and took a keen sense of pleasure from being a part of the family business. She was a fourth-generation jeweler and thanks to inherent talent and creativity, the Rossi name was synonymous with excellence. Unfortunately, with the exception of her father, she was the last of the family with any interest in continuing the traditional trade. Her younger brother, Sean, played guitar for a popular country-music band and traveled all the time, and her even younger sister, Bethany, was a professional student, happy with higher education and her job at the Gap. Neither of them were likely to change their minds.

Which just left her.

To complicate matters, her father had developed agoraphobia after the death of her mother. It had begun gradually. At first, he simply refused to travel. He'd said that his wife had always been his companion and he couldn't face going without her. Because her parents had genuinely been soul mates, Jess had understood and hadn't pushed him, assuming that it would only be temporary, that, in time, he'd be able to move forward.

She couldn't have anticipated how wrong she'd be.

Citing the need to "be closer to work," the second her new home, a tree house, was finished, her father had sold the family house in the country and finished an apartment above the store. Initially, Jess had thought this would be a good idea. The house was still a painful reminder of her mother, being in town would keep him from being lonely, etcetera. But it was when the apartment was complete that she really began to notice a difference.

Frank Rossi loved Shadow's Gap and the town square, where their business had stood for the past hundred years. He routinely ate at the diner next door and visited the other business owners around their little block. He'd played chess at the five-and-dime and shopped for all his clothes at Billy Walter's, an upscale men's store. He not only knew every proprietor, he knew their families, as well. He'd been social.

But shortly after moving into the apartment above the store, he'd started manufacturing reasons not to go out. He'd have the diner deliver his meals and he stopped visiting the other stores. He'd stand at the front door and look out, but when Jess had casually suggested that he go see if Billy had any new ties in stock, he'd shake his head and retreat to the backroom.

She'd begun to seriously worry at that point, but she hadn't realized how dire the situation had become until she'd discovered that Paula, one of their part-time workers, had been doing his grocery shopping for him. She'd also gone to the post office for him, picked up his prescriptions and generally did anything that would require a trip outside the shop.

At that point, Jess had confronted her father and had tried to get him to talk to a therapist, but her concern had been met with an uncharacteristic angry outburst and an order to mind her own business. He was fine, he insisted, though it was obvious that he wasn't, that he'd become a prisoner in his own space. He'd started spending an inordinate amount of time on the internet, his only window to the outside world.

It was then that Jess had started traveling for him— it would be good for her, he'd said—and, while most of the people her father had done business with over the years didn't think too much about the fact that he'd stopped doing the legwork, there were a few who did find it odd. One of those, a representative of the Mont-wheeler Diamond Company, made an unannounced visit to the store to share the news that Rossi's had made the final cut for the Clandestine design. When the man had asked her father to go out to celebrate and her fa-ther had declined, it was then that the older Rossi had become labeled a "recluse."

Interestingly enough, it was the "recluse" part that would seal his ultimate nomination for the Clandes-tine bra. Everyone assumed that her dad had retreated so far into his work that the outside world had become a distraction he couldn't afford and wouldn't indulge. It had given him a certain mystique that the press had instantly loved and capitalized on.

Their web hits had tripled and orders were pouring in faster than they could fill them. Even her own signa-ture line, If It Crawls, featuring bejeweled insects and bugs, had seen a significant bump in sales.

There was no doubt that the bra, much as it pained her to admit it, was already netting the results her fa-ther had expected. And it hadn't even had The Big Re-veal yet. Once it was covering the breasts of one of the world's sexiest supermodels, the buzz would really get going. And that was good for business.

In today's lagging economy, there wasn't a single company that wasn't affected in some way, theirs included. High-end jewelry was a luxury item and when money got as tight as it was now, fewer and fewer people had the ready cash to splurge on something like fine jewelry. They'd made good investments and her father had always been a big believer in gold, but they'd certainly had to tap into their reserves over the past couple years.

The Clandestine bra would change that.

And really, when one considered what was to gain, she really didn't have any business being put out over missing a race, one that she only wanted to run in order to prove a point.

With a quick glance at the clock, Jess sighed and closed up her garage, then made the quick walk through the woods to her place. She'd already packed, but still needed to shower and change. The security agent hired by Montwheeler was set to arrive at the shop at three to collect both her and the bra, and she'd promised her father she wouldn't be late.

If she intended to keep that promise, she'd better get a move on. She mounted the steps to her tree house— an eleven-hundred-square-foot architectural wonder of reclaimed wood and leaded glass—and leaped lightly over her cat, Pita (short for pain in the ass), who liked to lie on the next-to-last step, solely in order to better trip someone, Jess believed. Shorty had promised to come out and feed her while she was gone.

Thirty minutes later, she secured the house and lugged her bag to the car. Because she imagined the security agent was going to be either short on conversation or too long-winded to endure, she'd included her iPod and an eReader. For whatever reason, when she tried to picture the man, her warped imagination kept conjuring images of Kevin James from *Paul Blart: Mall Cop.* Why? Who knew, but it made her snicker every time all the same.

With a shake of her head and another glance at the clock—damn!—she slipped the key in the ignition and slung gravel as she peeled out of the driveway. From her house to the shop was ordinarily a fifteen-minute drive.

She'd need to do it in ten.

It was obscene how much that pleased her.

"WHAT THE HELL," Griff muttered, his gaze trained on the rearview mirror. He'd first noted the red Camaro—the retro-kind Chevy had debuted a few years ago—more than half a mile back when it had first appeared in the distance.

It was damn hard to miss.

Candy-apple red, white racing stripes from hood to trunk, and the way it had moved seamlessly in and out of traffic, smoothly passing everything that interrupted its path had certainly drawn his attention. A little admiration, even.

Now, as the car drew nearer to his bumper—so close that he could read the tag on the front, which appropriately read Faster—irritation was quickly dimming the original sentiment. He was moving five miles past the speed limit on a two-lane highway with a double yellow line. The driver couldn't pass without breaking the law, and he refused to go any faster.

Though he couldn't make out much beyond a lot of dark curly hair and sunglasses, he knew it was a woman behind the wheel and he'd admit, she seemed more than capable of handling the powerful, if impractical, car she drove. But if she didn't get off his damn bumper, they were going to have a serious problem.

He slowed a little, just to infuriate her. "I'm in front of you, lady. Get over it," he muttered.

She dropped back as they mounted a small hill, and Griff had just congratulated himself for making her retreat, when the yellow lines changed in her favor and she roared past him. He barely caught a glimpse of her pleased smile, but it was enough to make him want to hit the accelerator a little harder and take off after her.

Which was irrational, of course, so he put the thought firmly out of his mind. He was a grown man on his way to an important job, his first as a civilian. Playing cat and mouse with a girl—one who had a much faster car, no less—was a distraction he couldn't afford, and it rather startled him that he'd been inclined to do it in the first place. Chasing after her would have been pointless and, as a rule, he didn't pursue things he knew would be a waste of his time.

Feeling strangely unsettled, Griff watched the red car disappear over the next hill and released a pent-up breath. He drummed his thumbs against the steering wheel, suddenly restless, and shifted in his seat. He'd been on the road for almost eight hours already and knew that at least another four would be in his future today, if he planned to stick to his schedule. Which he did, of course, otherwise what was the point in having one?

He'd allotted eight minutes to pick up the bra and his Rossi escort, another seven for a bathroom break, and planned to arrive in Hagerstown no later than eight o'clock tonight. Dinner would be a little late, but not terribly, and that would put them within four hours of their ultimate destination. They'd hit New York City by noon tomorrow, which gave him a two-hour window to check out the venue before the press junket started. The bra would officially be on display—on the runway for the reveal—at noon on Saturday.

Payne had provided the building specs, which were certainly helpful, but Griff preferred to do an in-person review. He wanted to know every stairwell, elevator, exit and access point. He didn't expect any problems, but would be remiss if he didn't prepare for them anyway. Besides, he liked to be prepared. There was a certain comfort in knowing that things were in order.

Big, round hay bales lay in the fields on either side of the road and Queen Anne's lace and wild black-eyed Susans bobbed in the lazy breeze along in the ditches as he drove on. Nestled in one of the many valleys of the Appalachian Mountains, Shadow's Gap suddenly came into view, a quaint village of white clapboard houses, red bricked shops and well-manicured grounds. Though the leaves had begun to turn, fall hadn't quite gotten a foothold yet. Varying shades of green blanketed the hills rising up over the valley, creating a verdant landscape that would look perfectly at home on a postcard.

Following the signs for the Historic Town Square, Griff made the necessary turns and began scanning the various storefronts for Rossi's Fine Jewelry. It was then that he saw it, the red Camaro, and his pulse gave an inexplicable little jump.

Wonder of wonders, it was parked directly in front of the jewelry store.

Clearly "Faster" had a taste for the finer things. Irritatingly intrigued beyond reason, Griff took the empty parking space next to her car, then exited his Suburban and entered the shop. Though he automatically noted everything about the store—two workers, one old, one teenager, royal-blue carpet, rich wood-paneled walls, gleaming glass cases filled with equally gleaming jewels—*she* was what drew his gaze and held it.

At least the back of her, which was all he could see at the moment.

But it was enough.

She was tall with a slim waist and especially generous hips—which she needed to complement her extraordinarily lush ass—and long legs. She wore a thin-knit pink sweater, perfectly fitted jeans and a pair of worn cowboy boots, which had been embellished with vines and pink roses. Her hair wasn't merely dark or brown, but a deep decadent sable that didn't so much absorb the light as catch it, and it sprung from her head in a riot of big, wavy curls, then cascaded over her shoulders. It had energy, that hair. In fact, everything about her was vibrant, wholly alive, for lack of a better description.

His stomach gave an odd little jolt and a swift blaze kindled in his groin.

"I'm not late," she insisted to the older man, presumably Frank Rossi. "I arrived with a minute to spare." She huffed a breath. "Why on earth are you complaining? He's not even here yet."

"You've got to stop treating the town square like it's the track, Jessalyn," the older man said, as though he hadn't heard her argument. "Screaming in here on two wheels? It's unseemly. What would your mother think?"

She muttered something that Griff didn't quite catch, but whatever she said made her father frown.

Her father...

But if— Did that— But surely— *No worries, Major Wicklow. You'll recognize her soon enough.*

Oh, hell.

"And of course, he's here," Mr. Rossi told her, looking past his daughter to meet Griff's undoubtedly confused gaze. "He's a professional. Being late wouldn't do."

He heard her gasp, then she straightened and turned around.

The picture hadn't done her justice, Griff thought as a prickly heat spread from one end of his body to the other, then turned abruptly cold and made the return trek. He felt as if he'd been dipped in scalding water, then dunked in the Arctic Ocean, much like forged metal.

Naturally, only one part of his anatomy hardened.

The photograph could only depict so much—the shape of her face, the color of her eyes and hair—but it was the animation of the features, the sheer vitality of her being that couldn't be captured with something as mundane as a camera.

She *glowed*.

Her eyes rounded briefly when she saw him, then undoubtedly recognition dawned, and the corner of her lush mouth twitched. "Suburban, right?" she said, looking out into the street for confirmation. She didn't need it, though. She knew it was him.

"That's right," he said. "Though I'm surprised you remembered. You passed so many people this morning."

Her eyes twinkled in admiration at his vague little dig, and she gestured toward her father. "Dad appreciates punctuality."

Rossi snorted. "I appreciate a lot of things, for all the good it does me." The older man found Griff's gaze once more, then he hurried forward and extended his hand. "Frank Rossi," he said. "You must be Griffin Wicklow, of Ranger Security."

Griff nodded. "I am. It's a pleasure to meet you, sir."

Rossi glanced at his daughter. "This is Jessalyn, my oldest daughter and, as I'm sure you've deduced, she'll be accompanying you to the show."

Yes, Griff thought as he turned and offered her his hand, as well. He'd worked that one out within seconds of walking into the store. What he hadn't worked out was how he felt about it, though if he was hard

pressed to pick a predominant sentiment, *excited* probably worked better than anything else.

Alarmed was a very close second.

With a quirk of her sleek brow, her palm connected
with his. Though the ground didn't shake beneath his
feet, he felt some sort of internal quake all the same,
and a bizarre tingling rushed through his fingers. Her
hand was soft, her grip strong and puzzlingly, a line
of small calluses curled around the top of her palm,
nearest her fingers. Gratifyingly, her smile faltered a
bit and a hint of uncertainty lit her misty-gray gaze.

"Mr. Wicklow," she said with a nod, making the
opal dragonfly earrings dangling from her ears sway.
A matching larger pendant hung from a thin gold chain
around her neck, suspended between her breasts. He
envied the jewelry.

"Griff, please."

"Well, I imagine you're eager to get on the road,"
Rossi announced with a bracing breath, thankfully end-
ing the awkward moment. He gestured toward the rear
of the store. "If you'll just follow me, I've got everything all packed up and ready in the back."

Equally chagrined and concerned that he'd needed
to be reminded of their schedule, Griff nodded and
followed both Rossis behind the counter. While the
sales floor was immaculate and poshly decorated, the
back was less tidy and decidedly more shabby. The
heart-pine floors were scuffed from generations of
wear, faded wallpaper peeled in places from the walls
and, though he was sure there was some order to the
chaos—there had to be, didn't there?—there didn't

seem to be one designated work area. Tools and invoices and bits of metal, clasps and links of chain… they were everywhere.

Just looking at it made him twitchy.

Rossi ran his hands reverently over a black plastic case, then glanced up at Griff. "Would you like to see it?" he asked eagerly.

It would have been rude to refuse. "I'd love to."

The older man almost ceremoniously flipped the latches and then carefully lifted the lid, revealing what was inside. Though he hadn't expected to feel anything beyond dim curiosity, Griff found himself awed nonetheless. He felt his eyes widen and he instinctively moved forward, drawn in by the sheer beauty, to get a better look.

It didn't so much look like a bra as a work of art. Shaped like a butterfly, the body of the insect was a glittering stunner made out of various black stones, emeralds and rubies, as well as many other stones he didn't recognize. The wings were unbelievably detailed, with authentic-looking variations of colors and lines and flared out over the cups in a dazzling display of black, purple, pink, green stones, with row after row of diamonds inset to give it additional depth.

"Wow," he said, for lack of anything better.

Seemingly pleased, Rossi chuckled. "Two hundred hours in the design, more than a thousand in the execution. You're looking at six months of my life there," he said, "and the key to the continued success of the Rossi family tradition. Guard it well."

"Of course, sir," Griff responded.

"It's incredible, Dad," Jessalyn Rossi said, her voice soft with admiration. "Definitely some of your finest work."

The older man actually blushed. "You're the one who gave me the concept. And given the success of your own insects, as well as the fact that you're the heir apparent, I thought it was a good choice."

Something in his tone must have caught her attention because she stilled and looked up at him. "You make it sound like you're getting ready to retire."

He shrugged innocently. "Who knows? I might."

She rolled her eyes and gave an indelicate huff. "Yeah, right. I'll believe that when I see it."

Rather than respond, her father tucked the creation more firmly into the black foam that held it secure, then carefully closed the lid, snapped the latches and locked them with a key he produced from his pocket. He handed it to Griff, along with the case. "Jess has a spare key, in the event you need it."

Griff couldn't imagine why he would, but nodded all the same.

Jessalyn Rossi leaned over and gave her dad a hug. "I'll keep you posted," she told him.

"I have no doubt," he replied, a smile in his voice.

She withdrew and looked up at Griff. "I just need to get my things out of the car."

Griff nodded and, case in hand, followed her back out of the store. She quickly unlocked the car, then leaned in—giving him another unobstructed view of her lovely rear end—and grabbed a single suitcase and a purse. She straightened, then glanced over her shoulder and shot him a hopeful look. "I don't suppose you'd want me to drive?"

Griff smiled. "No, thanks. It's against protocol." He didn't know whether that was true or not, but it sounded better than when "hell freezes over." He was already feeling too left of center. Off balance. Allowing her to drive would no doubt compound the issue. As a matter of fact, he could safely say that he imagined everything about Jessalyn Rossi was going to compound the issue.

Because, God help him, *she* was the issue.

3

ER...SO MUCH FOR *Paul Blart: Mall Cop,* Jess thought as every hair on her body tingled with hypersensitive awareness. Honestly, when she'd turned around and saw him standing in the shop, a sonic boom of white-hot sexual attraction had blasted her so thoroughly it was a miracle she hadn't been blown backward, spread eagle, like something out of a superhero-comics movie. Her skin still felt singed from the heat, her middle a simmering muddled mess.

It was unnerving, to say the least.

A healthy twenty-year-old woman, Jess was accustomed to looking at the occasional handsome man and experiencing a passing whiff of feminine interest. The recognition would flit through her mind as quickly and unremarkably as a half-formed thought, one that was soon dismissed and replaced with something else. Her gaze shifted to her left and a shivery breath slowly leaked out of her lungs.

Griffin Wicklow was another matter altogether.

One whiff of him, so to speak, and she'd turned into the proverbial bloodhound. And if the hammering of her pulse and the tightening of her nipples were any indication, a female one, at that.

In heat, naturally, she thought with a droll quirk of her lips.

She couldn't have been any more stunned if she'd sprouted horns and grown a tail. *This* didn't happen to her. It had never happened to her, as a matter of fact. On the rare occasions she'd dated anyone long enough to segue into an intimate relationship—*rare* being the operative word, because oddly enough, most men didn't appreciate a woman who knew more about the engine under the hood than they did—desire had been something that had required…coaxing. Cultivating. A bit of persuasion.

It had never inexplicably slugged her across the middle with all the subtlety of a two-by-four.

It had never made her feel like icy fire had suddenly erupted beneath her skin.

More disturbingly, it had never made her nervous.

Being different had always demanded courage, so at this point in her life Jess could safely say that very little rattled her. And if it did, she'd eat glass and smile through the blood in her mouth before she'd admit it. She inwardly grinned.

It was part of her charm.

But the anxious energy presently twitching through her veins was something foreign and therefore more… concerning. She could literally feel him there, beside her, though they weren't actually touching. Every confident turn of the wheel beneath his wide, blunt-tipped beautiful fingers, each breath that moved in and out of his lungs, the slightest shift of his mouthwatering shoulder as he negotiated traffic.

It was madness. Sheer, utter, God help her, *thrilling* madness.

Perhaps he'd be willing to drop her off at the nearest hospital, Jess thought with a futile smothered whimper, where she could take advantage of some serious psychological help.

Clearly a lobotomy wouldn't be in order—she'd obviously already lost her friggin' mind.

But how could she not when he looked like *that?* If he'd been merely handsome or even just striking, she'd like to think that she would have momentarily swooned, but then recovered. After all, it wasn't as if good-looking men were that uncommon.

But fifteen minutes post meeting and she was still reeling, still toe-curlingly *aware.*

It was the hair, she ultimately decided. Curls did it to her every time. No doubt they were the bane of his existence and had garnered him endless teasing as a boy, but mercy, they were beautiful. Big and loose and messy, but easily styled as evidenced by a vague part that looked more as if a hand had done the work rather than a comb. And dark auburn, to boot, damn him. Her favorite color. Not quite brown, not quite red, but thousands of shades in between that caught the light.

The same color slashed boldly over eyes that were deeply lidded and equally riveting. Pinwheels of blue and green burst from his irises in wide, vibrant striations, as though Mother Nature couldn't decide which hue best suited him, so she gave him both in equal measure.

In direct contrast with the unforgiving masculinity of his face—the bold nose, mile-high, stark cheekbones, angular jaw—curly bronze-tipped lashes framed those remarkable eyes, a feature she was sure he resented. She was suddenly hit with the insane urge to touch them, those lashes, to feel the springy curve of them against the pad of her thumb.

Madness, she thought again, balling her hands in her lap.

One would think the Almighty would have been a little more considerate of the fairer sex when doling out Griff's finer features. For instance, because he'd been so liberal with his face, one would assume that, in fairness, Griff wouldn't have been blessed with so spectacular a body. Jess slid a covert peek over his long, muscled profile, her belly clenching when it reached his thigh.

Wrong.

It, too, was equally stunning, equally divinely made. At five-eight, Jess was a tall woman and therefore was accustomed to barely lifting her chin to speak to someone with additional height. This man easily topped six and a half feet and every inch of his physique was perfectly honed, devoid of any softness or, God forbid, fat, she thought enviously. It was a body that commanded attention from both genders, one that was fit and naturally conditioned. He moved easily in his skin, walked with an economy of movement that was as graceful as it was purposeful. He wore a cream-colored sweater, the sleeves pushed up to reveal fine copper hair dusting his forearms, and jeans that were worn and sat low on his lean hips. A little too low, she noted dimly, as though he'd recently lost a little weight.

Jess imagined most every woman longed for one forbidden encounter, to be bowled over by the shock of unadulterated sexual desire, the kind that resulted in torn clothing, whisker burn and hot, broken epithets in conjunction with even hotter, mindless sex. Many women imagined this sort of sex, casting an A-list Hollywood actor as their star performer, herself included, on occasion.

But move over, Channing Tatum, because Griffin Wicklow had just taken top billing on her imaginary marquee.

How extraordinary, she thought wonderingly. How electrifying. How...*stupid.* She inwardly sagged like a spent party balloon.

He wasn't just some random guy who'd inadvertently stumbled across her path and flipped her on switch—he was here in a professional capacity, to work, to protect her father's creation and guard Montwheeler's investment.

He was not here to play the starring role in her wild, frenzied jungle-movie sex fantasy. Assuming that he'd even want to, and that was debatable, at best. Her insecurities aside—and Lord knew they were considerable—Griffin Wicklow seemed too focused, too locked down, too *controlled* to engage in the sort of activity she was imagining. Not uptight, precisely, but—

she sent him another glance, searching for the right word—disciplined, Jess decided. Nature or necessity? she couldn't help but wonder, and for whatever reason, she knew she'd have to find out.

"Do you mind if we pull in at Sarah's Gas-N-Go there on the corner?" she asked brightly, pointing up ahead. "I need to make a pit stop and get some snacks for the road."

Predictably, the faintest flicker of a muscle jumped in his jaw. He cast a fleeting glance at the dashboard clock. "Of course. But make it quick, please. We're on a tight schedule."

Jess smothered a smile. Oh, she'd just bet they were.

He wheeled smoothly into the lot, drew up to the curb and shifted into Park.

"Aren't you coming in?" she asked.

"I'll wait."

All righty then. "Can I get anything for you?"

He shook his head. "I'm good, thanks."

Jess lifted a brow. "Not even a drink?"

"I've got bottled water in the back."

Of course he did. And most likely protein bars and a first-aid kit, because this man was nothing if not prepared. Mr. Efficiency. Oh, this was going to be fun. She grinned and opened the door. "Okay, then. I'll be right back." She sincerely doubted her interpretation and his of "right back" would coincide, but…

Jess took care of necessary business, leisurely filled a Big Gulp at the soda fountain, then ambled down the candy aisle. She was having the usual salty versus sweet debate when a shadow fell over her right shoulder and she felt him looming behind her. She squashed an irrational grin and the urge to squirm. She'd wondered how long it would take him to come in after her.

She turned around and smiled delightedly—innocently—up at him. "Oh, you changed your mind," she said, noting the case was in his hand. Diligent, naturally. She glanced back at the shelves, gave her head a little shake and winced thoughtfully. "I can't decide if I want Fiery Jalapeño Nachos or a Nutty Nougat Bar. What are you getting?"

"You," he said, his tone mildly grim. "Get both. We need to go."

Though he didn't touch her, she felt herded to the register all the same. Another odd little thrill whipped through her, churning her insides.

"Afternoon, Jess," Sarah said, nodding as she rang up her purchase. "How are you this fine September day?"

"I'm good. How are you? Hip feeling better?" The elderly Sarah had taken a fall from a ladder in the spring while cleaning out her gutters. At least, that's the story *she* told. Other members of Shadow's Gap had indicated that Sarah had taken a fall out of bed, and that Ryland Morris had landed on top of her.

Knowing Sarah, who was presently sporting enough cleavage to make Dolly Parton jealous, Jess was more inclined to believe the latter.

"It's still not at one hundred percent—hurts when rain's coming—but it's getting better." She idly bagged Jess's items, which made the man behind her twitch with impatience. "You're racing this weekend, right?"

Sarah continued. "Lane Johnson was in here this morning running his mouth again." She rolled her eyes. "That boy has too little sense and too much self-confidence. It's irritating."

Jess couldn't agree more, but didn't. "I'm not," she answered. "I'm actually on my way to New York. Business," she explained. "For Dad."

She felt him still behind her, could almost hear his antennae powering up.

Sarah inclined her head. "Ah. Well, that's a shame. Maybe next weekend then?"

"I'm planning on it," she said, handing over the correct change.

The older woman accepted the cash, then looked past Jess's shoulder, through the window into the parking lot. She winced and shook her head. "Looks like Monica Hall's got car trouble again, bless her heart. Honestly, when you're buying more oil than gas, it's time to get a new car."

Jess followed her gaze, spied the hood up on Monica's old Buick and bit her bottom lip. Monica Hall was a single mother of three whose worthless ex-husband hadn't paid child support in over a year. She couldn't afford to repair her old car, much less buy a new one. A nail tech at one of the local salons, Monica didn't miss an opportunity to work and was often at the store on Mondays, when everyone else took off.

Jess nodded her goodbye at Sarah, then turned and made her way out of the store.

"You were supposed to race this weekend?" Griff drawled, a gratifying hint of disbelief coloring his tone as he trailed along behind her. "Race, as in *a car?*" He snorted softly. "Faster," he muttered. "Why am I not surprised?"

Rather than head back to his truck, Jess started toward Monica. She handed him her purse and bag of snacks, which he accepted without so much as a blink. That distracted, was he? she thought, irrationally pleased. "Well, I'm sure as hell not running the fifty-yard dash, if that's what you're thinking. Monica?"

The young mother looked up from the engine, worry drawing lines that didn't belong on her otherwise smooth face. "Hi, Jess," she said. She gestured to the car, her expression hopeless. "Clementine's acting up on me again. Ordinarily, so long as I keep oil in her, she runs all right. I'm not sure what's wrong now. I can't get her to start."

Jess peered beneath the hood, inspected the oily engine, then dropped onto her knees and looked under the car. *Ah,* just as she'd thought. Oil dropped steadily onto the pavement, but that wasn't the reason the car wouldn't start. She grabbed a wad of paper towels from the dispenser. "The oil leak needs to be fixed or you're going to run into engine issues, but that's not the problem right now."

Monica crossed her arms over her chest to fight off the chill in the air. "It's not?"

"No, your battery posts are corroded." She winced. "My toolbox is in my car and this certainly isn't the best way to do it, but hopefully we can get her started." Using the towels, she cleaned as much of the corrosion off as possible, then straightened. "All right, Monica. Why don't you get in and give her a try."

"What kind of racing?" Griff asked. She could feel his curious gaze on her, lingering as though she was some sort of unknown species he'd stumbled across. It was disturbing, that scrutiny, the intense weight of his regard. Her palms tingled and she resisted the urge to push them against her thighs.

"Stock car," she answered, then smiled as Monica's engine caught and held.

Relief pushed a grin over the younger woman's face, erasing some of the premature lines, and she leaned out the car window. "Thanks, Jess! You're a lifesaver!"

Jess dropped the hood into place, then grabbed her purse from Griff's arm. He stared at it for a moment, seemingly stunned that he'd been holding it in the first place, then scowled comically.

Smothering the urge to laugh, she made her way over to Monica's driver's-side window and handed over her car keys. "My car is in front of the jewelry store. I'll call Dad and let him know that you're coming to get it."

Monica looked at the keys in her hand and blinked. "What?" She shook her head as Jess's meaning sunk in. "Oh, no. I couldn't—"

"I insist," Jess told her. "Leave your keys at the store and when I get back, I'll take Clementine out to the house and get that oil leak fixed for you. In the meantime, drive mine." She grinned at her. "It's just going to be sitting there for the next few days and—" she patted the roof of the car "—Clem needs a break."

Monica swallowed, clearly touched and torn, then

briefly looked away. "Jess, I appreciate the offer, but I don't know how I'd pa—"

"We'll work that out later," she said, waving her concern away. "Maybe trade it out in manicures?" She grinned ruefully and held up her hands. "These nails are always in need of help."

A tentative smile peeked around her lips. "Are you sure? I—"

Jess nodded decisively. "I'm sure. I'll give you a call when your car's ready, okay?"

"Thanks, Jess," Monica said, her eyes soft with sincerity. "I really appreciate this."

Jess knew she did. That's why she didn't mind helping her. "You're welcome."

Looking relieved and a little excited, Monica waved as she drove away.

Jess heaved a small sigh, then turned to find Griff staring at her, an inscrutable look on his handsome face. It was unnerving. "I know, I know," she said, plucking her snack bag from his hand as she started for his truck. "We need to go. We're on a schedule."

And for perverse reasons she wasn't certain she understood, she had every intention of wrecking it as often as possible. Because something told her that Griff Wicklow needed to learn to roll with the punches instead of holding too fast to his agenda.

It had to be exhausting.

4

GRIFF DIDN'T KNOW precisely when he'd become so jaded, but it was rare that anyone ever surprised him. Truly, genuinely surprised him. He'd taken one look at Jessalyn Rossi and, while every cell in his body had seemed to misfire and short out, he'd still thought he'd had her pegged. Pretty, creative, more than a little reckless.

Interesting? Definitely.

Hot? Without question.

A potential problem? Oh, hell, yes.

But watching her hand her keys over to the young woman at the gas station—keys to what was obviously a prized possession—and then offer to fix her car in exchange for manicures? That... He inwardly reeled.

That was something else.

Not to mention learning that she raced stock cars—and was missing a race this weekend to make the trip for her father—and knew her way around an engine well enough to know that the leak was coming from the valve cover gasket and not the drain plug or the filter. He knew his way around one, too. He'd worked part-time at a garage while in high school. He mentally grimaced. He'd worked *lots* of part-time jobs while in high school.

At any rate, Jessalyn Rossi wasn't just surprising—she was a revelation. One that he found as intriguing as irritating. He smothered a snort, glancing at her from the corner of his eye while she carelessly popped chips into her mouth and thumbed through a magazine. Every once in a while he'd catch a smile or a moue of distaste—she had the most interesting face—and it was a continual struggle not to stare at her, not to ask her the cause of each reaction. When, by all rights, he shouldn't care, shouldn't give six damns or a bloody hell. She was merely an accessory to the job at hand, a necessary inconvenience, a premature pain in the ass.

And yet...

An undeniably singular thrum of excitement vibrated through him, a bizarre sense of expectation tightened low in his belly—along with all the usual parts, of course—and it was with as much dread as anticipation that he admitted to himself that she was quite possibly the most fascinating woman he'd ever met.

He didn't have the time nor the inclination to be fascinated, Griff thought darkly. He had enough problems as it was—an image of his half brother Justin's hopeful smile surfaced at the thought, making him instantly uncomfortable—without throwing an inappropriate attraction into the mix.

They'd been on the road for the better part of an hour

and he'd made up the extra six minutes she'd cost them at the store by needling the speedometer a little farther to the right. The late-afternoon sun filtered through the window, backlighting her dark hair in a sepia-toned halo—a crooked one at that, which seemed strangely appropriate given what he'd observed during their brief acquaintance—and illuminated the side of her face, revealing delicate bone structure and a frankly sensual mouth. Because he didn't need to be thinking about her hot mouth and the things she could do to him with it, Griff decided a conversation was in order.

"That was nice," he said, his voice a bit rusty.

She looked up, a puzzled line appearing between her sleek brows. "What?"

"Loaning your car to the girl at the station."

Her expression cleared. "Oh, that," she said, as though she'd already forgotten the kindness. "Thanks. I thought she could use a little good luck." She frowned significantly. "She's certainly had enough of the other kind, poor thing."

"Oh?"

Jess casually flipped another page. "Her husband walked out a couple years ago. Left her with a set of twins and an infant. Conner and Cash were barely out of diapers, and Ava wasn't even a month old." Her face hardened. "Selfish bastard."

Selfish bastard, indeed, Griff thought, his anger spiking. He had enough experience with fathers who walked out to know what sort of hardship Monica and her children were going through. Jesus. Deciding not to be a husband was one thing—being a father wasn't friggin' optional.

Or at least, it shouldn't be.

He cleared his throat, hoping to dislodge the choking irritation building there. "I'd like to help out on the repairs for her car," he said.

She stilled and those pale gray eyes swung toward him. He'd clearly surprised her, a feat that he imagined was difficult to do. She looked away, back to her magazine. "That's not necessary. It's just the gasket. It's not an expensive fix."

Maybe not for the parts, but what about her time? Which begged another question—who taught her how to work on cars? He'd be willing to bet it hadn't been her father. The older Rossi seemed more interested in his jewels and gems than spark plugs and cables. An old boyfriend, perhaps? he wondered, irrational annoyance making his fingers tighten around the steering wheel.

"Be that as it may, I'd still like to help. At the very least, pay for your time."

She looked at him again, her focus more deliberate. "Why? You don't know Monica."

He smiled. "Do I have to know her to want to help her?"

She hesitated, studied him, evidently looking for some form of motive behind the offer. "No," she said finally. "I suppose you don't." She paused. "Thank you. I'm sure Monica will appreciate it."

"I imagine that's why you offered to help her in the first place," he said. She didn't strike him as the type to waste her time on ungrateful people.

Him, neither, for that matter, which had made giving his half brother, Justin, the kidney a little easier. He wouldn't have refused, of course—how could he when the boy had been handed a certain death sentence?—but knowing that Justin understood the sacrifice and appreciated the gift had made things much easier.

Or as easy as it was going to get, at any rate.

He could have happily gone the rest of his life without hearing from his father—he'd made it the past seventeen years, after all—and, though he'd known about Justin and had been periodically curious about the other boy his father *had* raised, Griff wouldn't have ever sought him out. It was too painful, for him, admittedly, but more so for his mother and sister.

Glory had been too small when their father had walked out to truly remember him, and Griff had always made sure to fill that role to the best of his ability. But his mother, while strong, had never fully recovered. She'd never remarried and, despite encouragement, only occasionally dated. But her heart hadn't been in it. Because, ultimately—even after all this time and all the pain—his father, the wretched bastard, still had it. Griff inwardly snorted.

If that was the so-called power of love, he didn't want any damn part of it.

And, much as he genuinely liked Justin, he didn't want any part of a relationship with him either. Strictly speaking, that wasn't true. He *would* like to get to know him better, would even reluctantly admit to a bizarre bond with the boy. But he couldn't afford to get to know him, couldn't put his mother and sister through that emotional turmoil, and protecting them was too ingrained in him at this point to change now. Someone had had to look after them when his father left and that someone had been Griff. They counted on him, depended on him. Going through the surgery had been difficult enough—separate waiting rooms for the families, set visiting hours to avoid running into each other. A nightmare.

It was over and done with, Griff thought. Six months post-op and all was well. Justin was healthy and out of danger, and his own recovery had progressed without complication. It was time to move on and the sooner Justin realized that, the better.

As if merely thinking of his brother had prompted it, his cell vibrated at his waist. Griff frowned, steeled himself before glancing at the display. Another text from the boy. Need some advice re: the bro code. Can I get a call back when you've got time?

He heaved an internal sigh. Not a demand, but a request. And a hopeful one at that. *Damn...*

Jess shifted a little in her seat and her soft scent drifted to him once more. It was something mellow and sweet, and strangely familiar. "Everybody needs a hand once in a while and, in my experience, it's usually those who need it the most who won't ask for it."

"So you do this often?" he asked, thankful for the distraction. "Trade goods and services for repair work?"

Her lips twitched with wry humor. "Too much according to friends, but—" she shrugged "—I enjoy doing it, and if it lightens someone else's load, then all the better, right?"

He nodded, impressed, and asked her the question that he'd been dying to ask for the past hour. "So... who is Lane Johnson and why has he been 'running his mouth'?"

She actually laughed, a light infectious sound that was pleasing to the ear. It was easy, that laugh, not the least bit affected. Her twinkling gaze swung to his. "Ah...I was wondering when you were going to ask."

Not if, but when. So she'd been certain? Had he tipped her off that thoroughly or was she simply used to the question? The latter, he hoped. He didn't like being predictable. It was...disconcerting.

She expelled a small breath, set her magazine aside, as though the explanation was going to require her full attention. She lifted her chin, her jaw firmed, and he perceived the slightest tightening around her eyes. "Lane Johnson is a fellow driver. He's loud and obnoxious and has a grossly misguided perception of his own skill. And he doesn't like it when a woman runs a better race than he does."

Ah... "Are there a lot of women who run a better race than he does?"

The corner of her lip lifted and she shot him a look, self-satisfied pleasure lighting her eyes. "Only one that I know of."

He chuckled. "You?"

"Me," she said, nodding once. "I smoked him on the last race—beat him by three and a half seconds— and since then he's credited the loss to a faulty carburetor and has been screaming for a rematch. He just can't accept that I ran a better race, that I—*a mere woman*—beat him."

Griff grunted. He knew the type. The military was full of them, but considering that women had just been granted the right to fight on the front lines of combat, those guys needed to get over it. He'd admit to having an exaggerated sense of protection when it came to women—particularly his mother and sister—and imagined that the impulse harkened back to cavemen days, when men guarded their women and dragged dinner home every evening. But any man who didn't appreciate a woman's strength was sadly misguided.

"He sounds like an ass."

"That's because he is." She pushed her hair away from her face. "And admittedly, there were a lot of them in the beginning. Stock-car racing is a predominantly male sport, so the resistance was there, of course. I was the butt of every 'woman driver' joke, I was bullied on and off the track. Typical chest-beating, ball-scratching guy stuff."

Startled by the ball-scratching comment, he felt his eyes widen and he choked on a laugh.

"But I stuck with it," she continued, darting him a concerned look. "I ran clean races—pushing back when I needed to—and I started winning." She looked away. "Then I was not as easily dismissed."

"Not easily dismissed" pretty much summed up his impression of her, Griff thought. He'd been wrong when he'd pegged her as reckless—*determined* was a much better description.

"So you earned their respect?"

"Everyone but Lane's," she said. "But I don't care whether I've got his or not." She scowled darkly, her brows furrowing. "I just want him to shut his mouth. More than anything, he's a nuisance."

There was a little too much bravado beneath that comment to take it at face value. Was she telling the truth? he wondered. Did she really not care what this Lane thought? Or was he the one person she wished to impress and couldn't?

For whatever reason, he found that thought less palatable than the first.

"He thinks that all his trash talking has scared me off, that I'm too afraid to meet him on the asphalt again. That's what he's telling everyone, anyway, and though I know it shouldn't—" she finished the sentence through gritted teeth "—it absolutely *infuriates* me."

"Really?" he deadpanned. "Because I would have never known."

The remark scored him a smile, which had been his intention, and as an a bonus he felt his own lips slide into a grin.

"Tell me it wouldn't make you mad," she said. "He's basically calling me a coward. I'll admit to being afraid of a few things—tight spaces, bats and clowns—but him? *Him?*" She snorted indelicately. "Not in the slightest."

He swiveled to look at her. "Clowns? Really?"

"Hey, don't judge," she scolded. "It's called coulrophobia and it's a lot more common than you think."

"You just made that up."

"I didn't," she insisted, laughing. "Look it up."

"So driving a hundred and eighty miles an hour around a track doesn't scare you but *clowns* do?" he asked, unable to keep the incredulity from seeping into his voice. He shook his head, equally shocked and amazed.

"That's right. Speed doesn't scare me—it's thrilling, actually. All that power beneath the hood, responding to my touch, to my instruction," she said, her gaze turning inward, her voice going low. "It's…incredible," she told him wonderingly. "The best feeling ever."

Right, Griff thought, feeling his dick shift at her almost sensual description. He swallowed, momentarily at a loss to respond. Thankfully, he didn't have to, because she smiled a little self-consciously and looked over at him.

"Sorry," she said, a light blush moving over her cheeks and, for whatever reason, he got the impression that didn't happen often. "I tend to get carried away."

"No apology necessary," he told her. "Better to be passionate about something than apathetic." And he admired that about her, that she'd risked the bullying and ridicule to do something that she so obviously loved. That took courage, a fearlessness that was becoming more and more extinct.

"What about you?" she asked. "What are you passionate about?"

Griff blinked, stunned and struck dumb by the question. What was he passionate about? *Him?* Honestly, he'd never really thought about it. There were many things that he liked—baseball, for instance. Alabama football—Roll Tide Roll. Getting sucked into a good mystery novel. John Wayne movies. Carrot cake, tuna casserole and naps. But was he actually *passionate* about those things? In the same way that Jess was passionate about racing? He shifted, suddenly uncomfortable.

No, he wasn't, he realized with a sickening sense of self-realization he wasn't eager to explore. He was not. He was not passionate about anything.

He grimaced, deflated and alarmed as an unhappy insight revealed itself—dear God…he was boring. Had he always been boring? he wondered. Or had this been a gradual development?

His gaze slid to Jess, her tall body practically shimmering with an inner energy, with an unmatched singular vitality. She waited expectantly for his answer, genuinely interested, it seemed, in his response. And suddenly he couldn't bear to tell her that he didn't have any passions, nothing that excited him—it was too damn pathetic—and he blurted out the first thing that popped into his head.

"Bull riding," he told her, startled at the inventive lie. It was impulsive and reckless—words he was certain no one had ever used to describe him—and insane. He'd never ridden a horse, much less a bull. Clearly he'd lost his mind, but it was too late now. He'd said it.

Her smoky-gray eyes widened in surprise—obviously she'd already pegged him as boring and this purely manufactured news didn't quite jibe with her estimation of his character—and she arched a slightly skeptical brow. "Bull riding? Really?"

He liked knowing that he'd shocked her. It evened

out the playing field a bit. "Oh, yeah," he said, nudging the speedometer another five miles over the speed limit. What the hell, right? In for a penny, in for a pound. "Nothing makes me happier than climbing onto the back of a two-thousand-pound angry animal whose sole desire is to throw me off and put a horn in my gut. Talk about a rush." Talk about bullshit, he marveled, amazed at himself.

While the suspicion hadn't completely faded from her gaze, an impressed smile had nonetheless turned her lips, making his ego high-five itself. "It sounds exciting. I hadn't pegged you for a cowboy."

He'd just bet she hadn't. "I left my hat and boots at the house."

"Yeah, you're not likely to have a lot of bull-riding opportunities in New York."

Small favors, Griff thought, laughing softly. "Right."

"It's a pity, though," she continued, her keen gaze still observing him. "I'd have liked to see that."

Panic punched his pulse more swiftly through his veins at the thought, then he stilled, belatedly discovering the brilliance of his lie. "You couldn't," Griff said, feigning regret. "Rodeo clowns."

One bullet dodged, he thought, wilting with relief, but he grimly suspected this would be the first of many.

5

I'M SORRY. IT'S nothing personal, old friend. Rest assured, I'll give it back.

Payne read the note again, experiencing the same little burst of shock when his gaze landed once more on the notorious signature. It couldn't be…could it? He shook his head, unexpectedly pleased even as unease curdled in his belly.

The Owl, or to the very few who knew the legendary thief's real name…Keller Thompson. An old boarding school friend, Keller had been frighteningly quick, excelled in absolutely everything and had often known more about the subjects being taught than the teachers themselves. Between the eidetic memory and the genius-level IQ, he always worked several steps ahead of everyone else and had made it look easy. Probably because it was, Payne thought.

But even being a genius hadn't spared him his father's wrath. While the majority of the boys at Payne's boarding school had had mean-bastard fathers, it was universally understood that Keller's was the worst. His father had yanked him in and out of school all during the year, and when he'd returned, it had often been with poorly disguised bruises and the occasional cigarette burn. School officials were required by law to report the abuse, but if they did—and that was a big if—nothing ever came of it. And though Keller had never confided in him, Payne had always suspected that there was something much more terrible than beatings going on with his friend.

Despite his unfortunate history, great things had been expected of Keller, so it was a bit of a shock when he'd basically dropped off the planet after graduation. Payne had tried to get in touch with him several times during college but had only succeeded once. The conversation had been as odd as it was brief and, beyond that, they hadn't spoken since.

He'd heard about him, of course, and had known instantly that whisperings of a notorious thief, whose calling card was a single owl feather, was his old friend. Keller had always had a thing for owls—the smartest predator, he'd always said—and the precision, ingenuity and bold way he went about his thefts had had his name written all over them. Or at least they did to anyone who'd known him.

But knowing it and being able to prove it were two completely different things, which was exactly what law enforcement and special government agencies all over the globe had learned. Keller had never had a single charge brought against him.

Not one.

And if his old friend was sending him a note of apology it could only mean one thing, Payne thought grimly—he was after the bra. Why? Who the hell knew? But it was the only thing in Ranger Security's protection that could possibly interest him.

Oh, hell.

Though most of their missions went off without a hitch, there were the occasional few that experienced unforeseen but manageable difficulties. Nothing that his agents had never been able to handle, of course— they were the best, after all. But Payne had a terrible suspicion that Keller's interest in their cargo was going to involve *much* more than a "manageable difficulty"... and that problem was going to land right at Griffin Wicklow's newly hired feet.

He'd better warn him, Payne thought. Then he'd contact the others and bring them up to speed.

Old friend or not, Keller would play hell stealing something under their protection.

ADMITTEDLY, MAKING SENSE of a one-sided conversation wasn't easy, but Jess had been able to glean enough information from Griff's increasingly scowling face and words like *thief* and *warning* to know that something was terribly wrong.

A pity, of course, because it had cut short her fanciful imaginings of his splendid, powerful body on the back of an equally powerful bull with long, curling horns. She'd mentally redressed him in boots, tight jeans, leather chaps and one of those Western shirts with the pearl snap buttons. And the hat, naturally.

A white Stetson, its only embellishment a braided leather cord.

She would have never pegged him for a bull rider—it seemed too unpredictable a sport for Mr. Control—and she wasn't altogether convinced that he wasn't simply yanking her chain, but ultimately, who was she to judge? She doubted there were many people who would have pegged her as a race-car driver, even though she spent most weekends tearing around the track. To each his own, she supposed, and it was certainly fertile ground for her imagination.

As if she needed more encouragement. She'd been practically squirming in her seat since the second her sizable ass had landed in it. He made her nerves jump and her blood sluggish, which was a very curious feeling. Not unpleasant, per se, but…different. Aware. Of him as much as herself.

"Right," he said. "Of course. I will not let it leave my sight." A pause, then, "Even as it goes on the model," he added grimly. "I agree, definitely the most critical time. In the interim, if you could send any information you have on him, I'd appreciate it. I'll go over it when we reach the hotel. We've got a couple more hours on the road before we stop for the night," he added. His blue-green gaze slid to her, making her pulse leap as it slid over her breasts, neck. "Well, so far. No, not an issue."

Oh, so they'd expected her to be an *issue,* had they? Jess thought, flattening a smile.

"Right, then. I'll be in touch later." He disconnected the call and muttered a low, heartfelt oath that betrayed what she imagined was the smallest fraction of his irritation. Intuition told her it was a rare occurrence and, for whatever reason, she suddenly felt sorry for him. It must be miserable being that tightly locked down, that unable to freely express oneself.

"Problem?" she ventured.

"A complication," he said, his voice tight. "Not a problem."

He obviously didn't allow "problems" in his world. "What sort of complication?"

He was quiet for a moment, obviously debating the merit of confiding in her versus leaving her in the dark, which was no doubt his first impulse. He made the right choice, ultimately, which prevented her from delivering a blow to the side of his head.

He studied the rearview mirror, hesitating. "My boss was just given advance warning from an old boarding school pal—who happens to be a notorious-but-never-caught thief—that he's going to attempt to steal the bra."

Jess had caught enough to know the majority of that, so she didn't linger on having her suspicions confirmed. Instead, she asked the most obvious question. She frowned. "Why warn us? What could possibly be gained?"

Griff thrummed a finger against the wheel, his body otherwise a statue it was so still. "Your guess is as good as mine. A warning gives time for preparation. Payne reckons it was for his benefit, because they knew each other." He laughed darkly. "And he's so confident that he's going to be able to take it from me that he's assured my boss that he plans to return it."

Jess blinked, mildly taken aback. "That does sound cocky. And illogical," she added. "Why steal something if you plan to return it? That doesn't make any sense." She felt her brow wrinkle. "Who is this guy again?"

He grimaced. "Someone called the Owl," he said dismissively. "I've never hear—"

She gasped. Griff's keen gaze swiftly swung to hers and narrowed.

"You've heard of him, then?"

Still more than a little stunned, she nodded. "I have, actually. He was rumored to be responsible for taking the Star of Midnight."

"Star of Midnight?"

"It's one of the largest sapphires in the world—around four hundred carats, if memory serves—and supposedly belonged in the Romanov collection. It vanished off the neck of an oil baron's wife at a party in Paris a couple years ago. One minute it was there, the next—" she snapped her fingers "—gone."

"Gone? How could it have been gone? Wouldn't that many carats have been heavy? Wouldn't she have noticed?"

"That was what was so brilliant," she said, turning more fully to face him. "He replaced it with a very well-done copy, one that was identical to the original in size and setting. Had he not attached a tiny owl feather at the clasp, it's doubtful anyone would have noticed the difference. A colleague of mine inspected it and said it was a remarkable forgery."

"So it wasn't enough that he took it—he had to let the world know that he'd taken it."

"That's the trouble with being a genius," she said, her shoulder lifting in a negligent shrug. "What good is it to be clever if no one knows you are?"

He shot her a speculative look, a hint of incredulity and disbelief rounding in his gaze. "You almost sound impressed."

That's because she was, reluctantly, at any rate. It was an odd sentiment to feel for a thief, she'd admit, but... "I admire the talent," she said, and winced regretfully. "It's a shame that he doesn't put it to better use."

He grunted, seemingly displeased, and looked away. "I wonder how much you'll admire his talent if he manages to steal your father's work."

There was that, Jess thought. She smiled at him, anyway. "But he's not going to, is he? Because you're not going to let him."

"Damn straight," he said with a determined nod.

"See," she said with a single, imperious nod. "Talent put to good use."

He offered her another sideways glance that whipped her middle into froth. "I don't want you to worry about this. I'll take care of it."

"I'm not worried," she told him, her lips sliding into a grin. "If you can handle a bull, then an owl certainly shouldn't be a problem."

And honestly, if anyone could keep the thief from taking the bra, Jess knew that it was Griffin Wicklow.

MAKING A VALIANT but appallingly unsuccessful attempt to ignore the fact that Jessalyn Rossi was naked in the shower—*naked* being the key issue, of course—Griff sighed through gritted teeth and redoubled his efforts to concentrate on the file in front of him.

Naturally, when he'd adjusted the plan to include a shared room—after all, she was under his protection now as well—he'd anticipated a little discomfort. Considering that he'd been semi-hard for the better part of six hours, he'd obviously been delusional when he'd made his original assessment. Because right now, between the raging erection and the images of hot, naked, wet skin, water sluicing between full rosy-tipped breasts, sliding in soapy rivulets over her ripe, bare ass—he jerked hard, swore hotly—he was more than a *little* uncomfortable.

He was freaking miserable, in the Best Possible Way Ever.

And she was absolutely off-limits.

He smothered a bark of ironic laughter, looked heavenward and shook his head. Just par for the course on this assignment, though, right? It wasn't bad enough that he'd been forced to travel with the single-most interesting and sinfully attractive woman he'd ever met—one who, impossibly, he wanted more than any other—fate had had to up the ante and give him a professional thief intent on stealing his cargo, as well.

And not just any thief either. A damn good one.

Though he'd initially scoffed at Jess's admiration of the Owl's talent, after reading the file and conducting his own search, Griff had to admit he was reluctantly impressed, as well.

If not in the act itself, then in the execution of it.

In addition to purportedly pulling off some of the

most high-profile thefts, this Owl person was a master forger, as well. Monet, Renoir, Picasso. Not only did it take an obscene amount of skill to competently fake those artists—brushstrokes, lighting, scale—there was the scientific aspect to it, too. He had to perfectly match the pigments to the time the masterpieces were painted, appropriately aging the artwork so that it not only looked authentic, but carbon dated correctly, as well.

And then there were the heists themselves. Never carried out in secret—he almost always worked within a crowd—they had a flair of execution that boggled the mind, as though he was performing some sort of magic trick and had an audience to please. Griff's lips twisted.

Oh, right. He did. The Hooters, just one of his many online fan clubs.

And it wasn't as if he was some sort of Robin Hood, stealing from the rich to give to the poor. There was no rhyme or reason to his thefts, no theme. Though he'd stuck predominantly to Impressionist artworks early in his criminal career, he'd clearly branched out since then. Paintings, small statues, jewels, even a jade hairpin from the Ming dynasty. And now the Rossi bra. Nothing linked them and, in the absence of a clear connection, one could only assume that what ultimately tied them all together was the oldest, most basic motivator of all…

Money.

He was a freelancer. And if that was the case, then who had hired him to take the bra? And, more significantly, why in the hell would he return it? Did he plan to steal it for the payout, then take it back and return it out of some sense of loyalty to Payne? That didn't make any sense. It could potentially ruin him, or at the very least cost him a few clients and affect his bottom line. Griff blew out a long breath and rubbed the bridge of his nose, heard the chirp of his cell phone, alerting him to another text.

Shit. Justin. He'd forgotten to call him.

Griff picked up the cell, fully anticipating another message from his half brother, but found one from his sister instead. Just checking on you. Don't push too hard, okay?

It was easier to agree than to give her the I'm-fine argument, so that's what he did. Then, confident that Jess was still in the shower and there wouldn't be an ounce of hot water left for him, he steeled himself and reluctantly dialed Justin.

The boy picked up on the first ring. "Thanks for calling," he said. "I wasn't sure you'd have time now that you've started your new job."

He expected so little, poor kid. "No worries," Griff told him. "What's up?"

Justin laughed nervously, then hesitated. "There's this girl," he said haltingly, practically blushing through the phone.

Griff chuckled. "There usually is," he told him. "What about her?"

"She used to date one of my friends, but they've been broken up for six months. Is it poaching if I make a move?"

Hmm. "How close is the friend?"

"He's a former teammate," Justin told him. "Definitely not one of my regular crew, but I've spent a lot of time with him on and off the field. Not that I'll be doing that anymore," he said, his tone more rueful now than bitter.

An all-star pitcher, Justin had been playing baseball since he was old enough to join a league, but the freak virus that had attacked his kidneys midway through his junior year had permanently sidelined him. At least as far as his mother was concerned, anyway. It sucked, and Griff couldn't help but feel sorry for him.

"But you see my problem, right? Derrick isn't a close friend, but ignoring him doesn't seem right either."

"Then don't ignore him. Let him know that you're going to ask her out, but don't let his reaction keep you from doing it. You should give him the heads-up, but if he and this girl—"

"Heather," he said.

"Right. If he and Heather have been over for six months, then in all probability, they're finished." A thought struck. "She's digging you, right?"

"I think so," he said, another nervous laugh echoing over the line. "She texts me a lot."

"Anything else? Does she smile at you? Has she suddenly joined any clubs or groups that you belong to?"

"She joined the bass-fishing team," he said. "Does that count?"

Griff laughed. "Bass-fishing team? I didn't know you were on the bass-fishing team." Hell, he didn't know there *was* a bass-fishing team.

"It was that or the debate team, and I decided I'd rather be on a boat than pressing a buzzer."

"Good call," Griff told him, still smiling. "So she joined when you did, then?"

"She did. And she's the only girl."

Griff settled more firmly against the headboard, and tucked an arm up behind his head. "Are you baiting her hook?"

He snorted. "No. Heather doesn't let *anyone* bait her hook."

He nodded, impressed. "She sounds like a keeper. And if she's followed you onto the bass-fishing team, then I'd say she's definitely digging you."

The bathroom door suddenly opened, a cloud of steam billowing out. A tangled mass of long, wet curls tumbling around her face, Jess emerged, makeup free and shiny-nosed, a look he found startlingly endearing. She'd donned the white hotel robe, which gaped open enough to reveal a bit of mouthwatering cleavage and accentuated her small waist.

She'd obviously caught the last bit of his conversation, because her ripe lips were curved into a slight smile and latent humor danced in her misty-gray gaze. She jerked a finger at her bag, indicating she'd forgotten some of her toiletries, then retrieved a wide-toothed comb and returned to the bathroom. She left the door open, presumably to let the room breathe, and he watched as she swung her hair over her shoulder and drew the comb down through the length. It shouldn't have been the least bit erotic—she was merely detangling her hair—and yet the sight of her, of her long, slender hands performing such a mundane but strangely intimate act was somehow the most arousing thing he'd ever seen.

He hardened to the point of pain, felt his throat close up, need and something else—something much more alarming—roared through him.

"Griff? You still there?"

He blinked, startled, the phone forgotten at his ear. "Er, yes. Yes, I'm here."

"So you definitely think I should ask her out?"

Jess pulled the comb through her hair again. "Yes, definitely."

"But not until I've told Derrick that I'm going to?"

Geez, he knew she had a lot of hair, but how long did this take? Sweat beaded his upper lip. "That's right. The bro code, remember?"

She shot him a look, mouthed "the bro code?" and arched a humorous brow.

"I remember." He blew out a relieved breath. "Right. Thanks, Griff. I knew you'd know what to do. Dad is useless at this kind of thing."

There was an undertone to his voice that Griff couldn't quite place, but it sounded familiar. Like disappointment and resentment. But that didn't make any sense—

"So where do you think I should take her? Should I do the classic dinner and a movie, or something else, something different?"

"Be different," Griff advised him. "But don't ask me how, because I don't know. It just needs to be something that you've thought of, that you've planned. She'll appreciate the sentiment."

"Do you have a girlfriend?" Justin suddenly asked, startling him. "It's just, you've never said."

"Not at the moment, no," he told him.

"A boyfriend then?" he queried, shocking Griff even further. "Because that's cool," he hastened to add. "Whatever makes you happy, bro—"

"No, not one of those either," he said, choking on a laugh. Jesus, this kid…

"Right. Well, I'll keep you posted on how things go with Heather. And if, you know, um…you ever need any advice, then I'm here for you."

I'm here for you. Griff swallowed, touched. "Sure," he said, clearing his throat. "Thanks."

"Talk to you soon."

Against his better judgment, more than likely, but yes, no doubt he would. He sighed, muttered a goodbye and disconnected. His gaze tangled with Jess's, sucking the air from the room, and the phrase "from the frying pan into the fire" suddenly sprang to mind.

Either way, he suspected a burn was forthcoming.

6

"Who was that on the phone?"

Justin started, his gaze swinging to the doorway where his mother stood. She'd lost more weight, he thought, noting the sharper cheekbones, the jeans hanging off her rail-thin frame. She always did this when his father left, lost her appetite, but it seemed worse this time. Like whatever food she did eat refused to stick to her bones.

He set the phone aside, leaned back onto his bed and picked up his remote control. "Not Dad," he said, knowing that was really the question she'd wanted to ask. "It was Griff."

"Oh, that's nice," she said, her eyes lighting with the first bit of pleasure he'd observed in a while. She tried to be happy, for his sake, he knew, but could recognize the difference between a real smile and one that was forced.

He hated his father for that, more than anything, for making her pretend that everything was fine when it wasn't.

Selfish, cheating bastard.

Initially she'd lied about his absences, had credited his father's long stretches away from home as part of his job, that traveling was necessary. It wasn't until Justin was twelve that he'd learned the truth, and only then because he'd stumbled upon it. He'd joined a travel ball team at the end of his regular season, hoping to keep his father around longer because, regardless of "work," he was never away during baseball season. In fact, his dad made every game, helped with practices, took him to the batting cages, the whole shebang. It was the only reason Justin had kept playing, really, to have his father home, his mother happy…to be a real family.

When his travel ball team had visited a park in a neighboring county, he'd spotted his father out with another woman at the restaurant where they'd stopped to eat after the game.

To his everlasting shame, everyone else had seen him, as well.

It had been *mortifying*.

He'd never forget the look on his father's face when he'd approached his table, watched his amorous player's smile capsize as recognition surfaced, then guiltily scramble away from the woman. She'd been young, with unnaturally red hair and a smear of marinara sauce on her chin.

"Working hard, huh, Dad?" he'd said, then simmering with rage and humiliation, he'd turned his back on him and rejoined his friends.

He'd never told his mother—he just couldn't bring himself to do it—and neither he nor his father had ever mentioned the incident again. But not mentioning it didn't lessen the knowing, and things had never been the same between them since. His father's drinking had escalated and his time at home had grown even more infrequent. And now that he'd never play baseball again, Justin knew that seeing him regularly was unlikely.

His mother knew it, too, but wasn't ready to accept it yet.

"How is Griff?" she asked. "Still doing well?"

"Yeah, I think so. He's started a new job, so he doesn't have a lot of time to talk."

His mother took a seat on the edge of the bed, laid a hand on his arm. "I'm sure he has time to talk to you," she said. "You're family."

"Not really," he said, wishing the words didn't hurt quite so much. "His mother is his family. Glory is his family." His lips twisted. "I'm just some shared DNA whose existence wrecked his childhood and ruined his career."

His mother inhaled sharply and squeezed his arm. "That's not true," she said, frowning fiercely. "Your father made the decision to leave Griff's mother, to cut all contact. That's not your fault. It's his," she insisted.

"He left Griff's mother because you were pregnant with me."

Had she forgotten that he knew the truth? That all of it—the whole horrible tale—had come out when his kidneys failed? When they'd had no other choice but to contact his half brother and sister to see if either one of them would be a match? Had he not gotten sick, he'd have never known about them, never even known they existed.

But they *had* known about him...and never made an effort to contact him. He swallowed, his throat tightening with disappointment.

"I didn't know that he was married, Justin," she said, sighing wearily. "And by the time I did, it was too late. I've explained this, as best I can already. I encouraged him to see Griff, to see Glory, to at the very least send some support to Anne-Marie." She shook her head, her gaze turning inward. "But he wouldn't do it. You know how your father is."

Yes, he did. He was a shitty husband, and an even shittier father.

Maybe that's why it was so important for him to get to know Griff, so that he could show his brother that he wasn't like their father, that he'd been worth saving, that he'd been worthy of the sacrifice he'd made for him.

That it wasn't his fault.

And as far as big brothers went, Griff was definitely the jackpot. He'd been an army ranger, for heaven's sake. A straight-up badass. He was brilliant, tough and above all else, steady. If he said he would do something, then he did it and, after living with a man who broke promises faster than he made them for the better part of his life, Justin had to admit, he found that quality the most admirable of all.

Though Griff wasn't on Facebook, Glory was, and Justin had pored over her page, looked at all the posts and pictures, several of which had included Griff. Glory often talked about him, about how wonderful he was, even called him her "rock."

To be fair, his mother had always been his rock, the one person he could count on, so he didn't necessarily need one of those...but a brother would be nice. And a sister, too, of course, though admittedly he felt closer to Griff. How could he not, given the surgery? Given the fact that Griff had saved his life?

"You hungry?" his mother asked, snagging his attention with the subject change.

He was, actually. He lifted a hopeful brow. "Do we have any tuna?"

She blinked, seemingly astonished, then laughed. "Tuna? Since when do you eat tuna? You've never been able to stand the smell, much less eat it."

"I don't know," he said, shrugging. "I've just got a craving for it." He'd had a few others as well, like carrot cake when his favorite had always been red velvet. It was odd.

"All right, then. How about I make you a sandwich?"

Justin aimed a hopeful smile at her. "How about you make a casserole so there's enough for both of us?" She needed to eat as well and he intended to make her match him bite for bite.

She stood, a ghost of a grin on her lips. "Casserole it is, then." She walked to the door, then paused and turned around to look at him. "Keep checking in on Griff," she said. "It had to be hard for him, hearing from your father after so many years, but you're not his father—you're his brother—and I'm sure he'll come around."

Then she obviously knew more than he did, Justin thought, because he wasn't nearly as certain.

One could hope, though, and he did. He really, really did.

THOUGH SHE'D NEVER admit it, Jess was actually mildly relieved that Griff was the one behind the wheel as they drew closer and closer to the city. Traffic was a snarled-up mess, lanes were only used as suggestions and she'd seen more single-finger salutes this morning than she could ever recall. She inwardly shook her head. Insane. She cast a glance at her driver—razor-sharp cheekbones, chiseled jaw, auburn curls—and felt heat bloom beneath her skin, concentrate in her nipples, as desire slammed into her once again.

You'd think at this point she'd be used to it, Jess thought, that prolonged exposure would lessen the reaction, but…no. If anything, heaven help her, it was worse.

How could it not be after last night?

Hour after hour of listening to him breathe, the faintest rustle of sheets when he'd move, and there'd been something particularly stirring—intimate, even—seeing his long muscular leg slung out from beneath the duvet this morning. Of course, if she hadn't drooled at the sight of his bare chest last night when he'd walked out of the bathroom after his shower, then seeing his mere leg shouldn't have been a problem. She bit her lip, squashed a sigh, remembering.

Her imagination, which she liked to think was more than adequate, hadn't done his body justice. It had miscalculated the breadth of his shoulders—impossibly, they were wider—and hadn't fully anticipated the scale or delineation of his muscles. His pecs were broad, the muscle curving just so, making his nipples cant at a mouthwatering, purely lickable angle, and his abs were so perfectly proportioned that if she'd seen him in a magazine, she would have sworn by all that was holy that they were airbrushed on.

A smattering of copper hair dusted his skin, then formed a tight line and slid low. She'd noted two small scars on his abdomen—war wounds? she wondered—and had been curiously moved and heartened by the minute imperfections. It didn't seem fair that he wouldn't have any. Additionally, she'd glimpsed a tattoo on his shoulder, a single Latin phrase written in a pretty, scriptlike font—*facta non verba*—which she'd used her cell phone to translate.

Deeds, not words.

A noble sentiment to be sure, but significant enough to ink permanently on one's body? As an ever-present reminder? Significant enough to him, evidently, Jess thought. Which naturally begged the question…why? Were they just words to live by? Or was a broken promise to blame? Considering how seriously and deliberately he did everything—case in point, the bra had gone into the bathroom with him last night—she imagined the tattoo was a combination of both, leaving her with even more questions. Intuition told her he wouldn't give up the answers easily, but then when had that ever stopped her?

His cell chirped from the cup holder—something

it had been doing the majority of the morning—and she watched him glance at the display, his lips form a whisper of a smile.

"Your boss again?" she asked, knowing that it wasn't. He'd scowled each time he'd received a message from Ranger Security. The last call had been from someone named Charlie, who'd given him the grim news that their supposedly impenetrable computer system had been hacked and that the hacker had "hooted" at her. Her outrage had echoed loudly enough across the line that even Jess had heard it.

"No," he said.

And that was it. He didn't offer more. Just...no. It was infuriating.

"Girlfriend?" she queried.

He offered another faint smile, one that was somehow sexier than the last. "No."

So no to the question, but not to whether or not he had a girlfriend? She resisted the urge to grit her teeth. All right, then. Hardball time.

She arched a brow. "Mother or father? Brother or sister? Granny, grandpa, aunt, uncle, cousin? Friend, enemy or acquaintance?"

He chuckled, his eyes widening at the barrage of questions, seemingly surprised at her persistence. "Strictly speaking, none of the above."

Jess sucked in an outraged breath and leaned closer. "That's not possible. I've listed every potential connection."

"Clearly you've done this before," he drawled, his

mouth still curved into that panty-melting half smile. "You know, since you've put so much thought into it."

She had, actually, but what difference did that make? She leaned back into her seat, picked a tiny piece of lint from her slacks. "I like to know things."

"Things that aren't any of your business?"

She grinned, not the least bit repentant, and shrugged. "*Especially* those things. Oftentimes I find they're the most interesting."

A bark of laughter burst from his throat. "The most interesting?" he parroted, shaking his head. "You're—" He struggled to find the right word, one that would fit her description, without being insulting, she imagined.

She took pity on him. "Honest," she finally supplied.

He laughed again, the sound deep and low. It was nice, that laugh. Genuine and steady.

It wasn't always that way. She'd once been set up on a blind date with a guy who was quite good-looking, but laughed like a little girl who'd taken a hit of helium first, staccato and high-pitched. It was creepy, that babyish girlie sound coming from a grown man with day-old stubble. She inwardly grimaced. Needless to say, it had been a deal breaker.

"Honest works," he said magnanimously, nodding wonderingly as though he was still unsure of what to make of her.

"So?" she prodded.

"So what?"

"The text?" she reminded him.

"Oh, right." He checked the rearview mirror, something he'd been doing frequently since they'd left the hotel this morning. "It was my half brother. Justin."

Ah, she thought, inclining her head. Half brother— not technically a brother, but close enough. "Is that who you were talking to last night?"

She'd wanted to ask at the time but had been side-tracked with talk of the Owl and all his exploits. They'd spent the better part of an hour going over the files Ranger Security had forwarded to him, as well as doing their own internet searches. Given the thief's practi-cally legendary status, Jess knew that she should prob-ably be worried, but strangely enough…she wasn't. Whatever happened—whether the bra was ultimately stolen or not—she knew that Griff would move heaven and earth to protect it, or if need be, to get it back.

Deeds, not words, she thought again. The phrase perfectly described her security expert. He was a for-mer ranger. She'd learned that last night, when he'd been extolling the virtues of his firm and all the rea-sons why she shouldn't be concerned with the so-called threat against the bra's safety. She hadn't thought about it then—she'd been too distracted with other things, like the shape of his mouth and the Owl—but now she wondered… What had made him leave the military? Was he burned out? Tired of war? Or did it have some-thing to do with those scars she'd noticed last night?

From what little she knew about the military, the men who went through the grueling process of Spe-cial Forces training were typically the ones who were committed to their careers, the soldiers who put in their twenty years, then retired and went to work in the private sector or for the government. They didn't simply *exit* without good cause. Her speculative gaze slid to Griff.

And this one certainly wouldn't have done so.

More questions, Jess thought. He was a bona fide mystery man.

"What's makes you think I was talking to Justin?" he asked.

"Because you mentioned the 'bro code' and were giving him girl advice," she said. Rather good girl advice. She'd been impressed and said as much. "You were right. Girls do appreciate that kind of sentiment, like knowing that a guy's thought about what would make her happy."

He shook his head, seemingly further mystified by her behavior. "You caught every word, didn't you?"

"Not on purpose," she said, feeling a bit defensive. "But I couldn't just go deaf because you were on the phone. If you'd wanted privacy, why didn't you go out into the hall?"

He'd been too busy watching her comb through her hair, that's why, and she knew it. She hadn't opened the bathroom door to give him any kind of show, though admittedly his lingering gaze had been gratifying. She'd opened it because the overhead fan had been broken and she'd needed some cooler air. And after he'd watched her—the weight of those glorious smoldering eyes following her every move, sliding along her body—she'd needed more than cool air, she'd needed a cold shower.

Mercy.

It was going to be a miracle if she got through the next few days without embarrassing herself. Or having some sort of psychotic break due to chronic, intense sexual frustration.

"It *was* Justin," he grudgingly admitted. "And, yes, he'd asked for my advice."

She smiled, pleased that he'd finally answered her. "He's younger, right? Your tone had the older-sibling ring to it," she added. "That's something I've got a good deal of experience with."

"You're the oldest?"

"I am. There are two years between me and my brother, and four between me and my sister. One or the other is always calling about something, though usually it's Bethany. Once the baby, always the baby," she said with a fond sigh.

The corner of his mouth twitched. "Sounds like my little sister."

So he had a sister, as well? But she wasn't a half, or he'd have made the distinction. "How old are your siblings?"

If she hadn't been watching him so closely, she would have missed the slightest tightening of his jaw and the effort it took to relax it. How odd, Jess thought, feeling a strange tension hover around him. Much as she liked to know things, she wasn't in the habit of introducing subjects—or pressing them, for that matter—that were a source of pain. Griff didn't looked pained, per se, but this was clearly an area of his personal life he didn't relish discussing. She'd just opened her mouth to tell him to forget it, when he spoke.

"Glory is twenty-one," he said, narrowly avoiding a biker who'd swerved into their lane. "She just graduated from nursing school."

"That's quite an accomplishment. You must be proud of her."

"I am," he said. He let out a small, almost bracing, breath. "Justin is seventeen and I've known him less than a year," he said levelly. "But I probably wouldn't have known him at all if he hadn't needed my kidney."

JESS GASPED SOFTLY and her eyes widened in shock, before melting with admiration and concern. He was hard pressed to decide which sentiment affected him the most. Or why *she* should affect him, when no one else had.

"Your kidney?" she breathed. "You gave your brother your kidney?"

Griff had no idea what had prompted his admission to her when he'd been doggedly silent on the subject with everyone else, but there it was. He'd done it. Whether it was the long hours trapped in the car with her, the longer night when he'd been achingly aware of virtually every breath that moved in and out of her lungs, or her simple "I like to know things" confession that he'd found refreshingly glib, he couldn't say. He just knew that he could tell her—*wanted* to tell her—which was as liberating as it was terrifying.

He nodded. "Six months ago."

"Ah," she breathed knowingly, as though something had just occurred to her.

"What?" he asked, sliding her a suspicious look.

"The scars," she said, gesturing to his abdomen as a blush rose on her cheeks. "I, uh, noticed them last night."

She had, had she? Griff thought, pleased to know that he wasn't the only one who'd done a little looking. And those scars were negligible, little more than scratches, really. She had to have been looking quite closely to notice them. He felt a smile move over his lips, knew that more than a smidgen of masculine pleasure clung to it, as well.

Her color deepened and she looked away.

"So he's fine, then? Your brother?"

"He is." He explained what happened, how Justin had gone from being a healthy teen—an all-star baseball player—to deathly ill in a single week. "It was bad. Dialysis was a stopgap measure, but it wouldn't have worked long term. His kidneys were too damaged from the virus."

"He's lucky that you were a match," she said. "And only seventeen." Her speculative gaze swung to his. "That's a pretty big age gap between the pair of you."

An image of his father's car as it disappeared down their old street surfaced and he beat it back, along with the bitterness and frustration it brought with it. "Twelve years. Justin was born less than six months after my father left."

She scowled. "I don't like your father."

Griff chuckled at both her expression and her comment. "Neither do I."

"I'm sorry," she told him, shooting him a repentant look. "I shouldn't have said that."

"No worries," he assured her. "There's not much to like. I hadn't spoken to him since the day he left until he contacted me about Justin. Neither of them—Dad and Priscilla, his latest wife—were a match. If either of them had been, I'm certain I wouldn't have ever heard from him again."

She was quiet for a moment, her jaw momentarily locked tight. "So is that why you left the military? To do the surgery?"

He nodded. "I could have stayed, but I wasn't sure what my future would have looked like. I'd be driving a desk or training, more than likely, and that's not my style. Besides, my mother and sister had been hounding me for years to come home." He shrugged. "It seemed like the right time."

She grunted under her breath. "It doesn't sound like you had much of a choice."

He hadn't, really, but ultimately, what difference did that make?

She lifted a brow. "Your sister wasn't a match?"

Traffic inched along as they entered Times Square, making him twitchy and impatient. "She was never tested. Once I'd been deemed a viable donor, there was no point."

She stared at him for a long moment, her ordinarily open gaze curiously closed and unreadable. Finally, she swallowed and when she eventually spoke, her voice was raspy and not altogether steady. "You're a remarkable man, Griffin Wicklow. I hope your family appreciates the sacrifices you've made for them."

He shifted, uncomfortable with the unexpected praise, and looked away. "I only did what anyone would do."

She shook her head and smiled sadly. "I don't think so. It's easy to do the right thing when there's no personal cost," she said. "But doing the right thing when the price is more than just an organ, it's a career? A way of life? An identity, even?" She caught his gaze, held it, making his heart kick hard against his rib cage. "That's extraordinary."

She got it, Griff thought in amazement, an odd airy vibration resounding through his middle. When no other woman, least of all his mother or sister, had understood what coming out of the military had meant to him, this woman—who'd known him less than a day and with fewer facts—genuinely got it.

That was extraordinary. *She* was extraordinary.

And, as he wheeled the SUV into the hotel driveway, watched as red-clad valets hurried forward to assist with their exit, Griff knew without a shadow of a doubt that he was in trouble. In fact, he could safely say that the Owl was the least of his worries.

Jessalyn Rossi, on the other hand, posed an imminent threat.

7

THANKS TO THE skinny, mostly braless models littering the lobby of the hotel, Jess was keenly aware of the additional bulk on her ass and tried to compensate by sucking in her stomach as she and Griff made their way to the check-in counter. Because she was fully under his protection now as well, she'd been forced to resign herself to rooming with him last night, so hearing that the same arrangement was in place now that they'd arrived in New York wasn't a surprise.

Finding out that they'd been booked into the honeymoon suite, however, was.

"The honeymoon suite?" she hissed at him before he could respond. "Really?"

She seriously doubted there'd be two beds in the damn honeymoon suite. Sleeping in the same room was difficult enough, but sleeping in the same *sheets?* Her mouth parched at the thought and her pulse hammered with panic as it moved faster and faster through her veins.

Sleek bare skin, muscles and masculine hair, auburn curls against a blindingly white pillow...

Griff leaned forward, his smile tense. "I think there's been some sort of mistake," he said. "We're supposed to have a two-bedroom suite. My boss called earlier and made the requested changes to our reservation."

The clerk stroked a few keys, regarded the computer screen, his brown brow furrowed thoughtfully. "Ah, yes," he said, his voice reminiscent of an island accent. "Here's the notation. Mr. Payne *did* call, but upon reviewing our availability decided that the honeymoon suite offered the best location in the building for your purposes."

Griff's gaze sharpened. "It's on the sixteenth floor?"

The clerk nodded. "Shall I key your cards now?"

Jess didn't know what was so significant or special about the sixteenth floor—some safety measure, no doubt, which made it the most desirable—but despite her racing heart and mounting panic, Griff accepted the suite and, looking equally grim-faced, followed her onto the elevator. The doors closed, leaving them alone once again. Before an uncomfortable silence could fully stretch between them, George Michael's "I Want Your Sex" sounded from the interior speakers.

Really? Really?

Jess felt her eyes round and cast a conspicuous look at Griff, who was looking heavenward, an I-can't-believe-this expression on his tense face. His jaw was clenched so tight it was a miracle she couldn't hear the enamel grinding off his teeth. A teenage couple joined them on the third floor, smiled significantly at each other when they heard the music, then really got into the spirit of the song and started making out.

Enthusiastically.

Loudly.

Honest to God, Jess thought, squeezing her eyes shut to avoid looking at them. She hadn't heard that much slurping since the watermelon-eating contest at the Shadow's Gap Town Festival last summer.

By the time they finally arrived at their floor, her nerves were stretched to the breaking point and the girl's skirt was riding high enough on her ass to reveal a Tigger tattoo and no evidence of underwear. When the doors opened, Jess darted forward like a spooked horse let out of the gate, Griff hot on her heels.

He shot her a look, his mouth sliding into a relieved half smile. "Good grief," he said. "Where's a hose when you need one, right?"

Jess returned his grin. "I don't think it would have made a difference," she said. "In fact, they probably would have liked it. Wet 'n Wild in the elevator."

He grunted in response, inspected both ends of the hallway, then double-checked the room numbers against his key card before turning right away from the elevators. Fully in his element, he held tight to the case and scrutinized every inch of their surroundings—stairwells, windows, the ceiling, the proximity of the other rooms as they approached theirs.

Anxiety tightened in her belly and she found herself holding her breath as he pushed the key into the lock and opened the door for her. His gaze caught hers and there was something equally endearingly and tortured in his, as though he found the idea of sharing a glorified Sex Room with her just as stressful. Though she'd noticed that he, at the very least, found her attractive, it wasn't until that instant that she realized he wanted her. It was there in his gaze, the stark need, the hopeless desperation. She sucked in a startled breath.

Oh.

Oh, wow.

How in the hell had she missed that? Jess wondered, inwardly reeling with joy and feminine pleasure. Had he disguised it that well? Or had she merely been so blinded by her own lust that she'd failed to notice his? Probably a combination of both, she decided.

He blinked then, seemingly disturbed that she'd seen too much, and nudged her forward with a finger to the small of her back. That simple touch sizzled against her spine, spread a thrilling warmth through her limbs, which only seemed to intensify as she walked into the room.

Good Lord...

For whatever reason, when she thought of a honeymoon suite, images of black lacquer furniture, red satin, a heart-shaped tub and a champagne tower immediately sprang to mind.

This honeymoon suite, however, was nothing like her imagination—it was...breathtaking.

Antique-reproduction, cream-colored gilt-edged furniture populated the room, most especially the enormous four-poster canopy bed, which was visible from the open French doors. The walls were covered in sky-blue watered silk, then gave way at the ceiling to a hand-painted celestial scene of naked cherubs, fluffy clouds, various birds, twining greenery and ribbons.

A huge, heavily carved white marble fireplace—were those dogwood blossoms?—stood between two of the lushly draped floor-to-ceiling windows and a merry blaze flickered from the hearth. Plush creamy carpet blanketed the floor in the living room and bedroom, then gave way to dark hardwood in the dining area and marble tile in the small kitchen. Vintage gold-and-crystal sconces flickered light around the room and gilt-framed artwork of various half-naked couples and garden landscapes provided richness and color to the palette.

A bottle of champagne waited in a silver bucket on the coffee table, along with a pair of gold-edged flutes and a plate of chocolate-covered strawberries and sugared pineapple. Huge bouquets of fresh flowers were scattered around the rooms and perfumed the air—roses, peonies, gardenias, lavender and heliotrope.

The suite was luxurious and romantic, intentionally overdone but tasteful.

Obviously every bit as stunned as she was, it took Griff a full thirty seconds to remember his job and go into security mode. Rather than get in his way, Jess took the opportunity to investigate the rest of the suite. The kitchen was stocked with a variety of drinks, snacks, a meat-and-cheese tray and a bowl of fresh fruit, and the bathroom was every bit as awesome as she'd expected. Heated floors and towel bars, a huge glass shower with multiple heads and the pièce de résistance, a massive marble jetted tub, surrounded by Greek columns and an inset fireplace and television.

Griff walked in, then stopped short and whistled low.

Jess smiled and arched a brow. "Impressive, isn't it?"

"It is," he said, sidling forward to pick up the remote control.

Out of everything that was in this suite, naturally it was the gadgetry that would appeal to him. She smothered a snort and an eyeroll, and watched him inspect the buttons, then turn on the fireplace.

He beamed, pleased. "That's handy."

Jess fingered a thick towel. "Is a custom bathroom with a fireplace and a television in your future?"

"It could be," he said. "Payne did say I could do whatever I wanted to with the space."

Jess frowned. "You live with your boss?"

He laughed. "No, I have an apartment in the building. Most of the agents do," he added, then turned on the television...which evidently defaulted to the adult-content channel, because an image of a brunette with her painted lips wrapped around a massive penis suddenly filled the giant screen.

Jess let out a startled little squeak.

Griff fumbled the remote and swore, frantically mashing buttons until the television turned off. "Sorry," he muttered hoarsely. "I, uh, I..." he stammered.

She'd done more blushing in the past twenty-four hours than she had in her entire life, Jess thought, feeling the sting of heat climb her neck. "Aren't those ordinarily part of the pay-per-view service?"

He cleared his throat, carefully set the remote aside and walked over toward the shower. "It's complimentary with the suite," he said, his voice still a bit strangled.

She crossed her arms over her chest, nodded once. "Oh."

He still hadn't looked at her. "Inspiration for the honeymooners, I reckon."

She felt a droll smile curl her lips. "One would hope that honeymooners wouldn't need any inspiration."

She certainly didn't. In fact, if she were any more *inspired* she'd be in serious danger of self-combustion. She nervously tucked her hair behind her ear, tried to think of something besides how Griff would taste against her tongue, how he'd feel in her mouth. Her belly melted into a muddled mess and an achy heat swept through her loins, making her resist the urge to squirm. Her nipples beaded behind her bra, ruching into sensitive peaks that craved the rasp of his tongue, the warmth of his mouth. Her hands shook and she clasped them together to disguise the tremor.

He still hadn't turned around, was still pretending to look at the shower. He had a white-knuckled grip on the case and his shoulders were tight with tension. She caught his profile when he shifted and noted the immovable line of his jaw, the firm set of his lips.

Clearly, he was mortified, and her continued presence seemed to be compounding the issue. Rather than make things worse by prolonging the awkward porn discussion, she jerked her finger toward the bedroom and headed toward the door.

"I'm just going to go ahead and put my things away," she said haltingly.

He nodded. "Excellent. I need to...uh, make sure this area is secure."

Jess frowned. There was only one door and no windows, so she didn't know how it couldn't be "secure," but inclined her head all the same.

How sweet that he embarrassed so easily, she thought with a small smile. He was truly one of a kind.

And he wanted her.

The only question that remained was...what was she going to do about it?

MONUMENTALLY RELIEVED THAT she'd left the bathroom, Griff gritted his teeth and glanced helplessly at his crotch, willing the stubborn hard-on to recede. He'd been playing mind games with his dick for hours, conjuring images of gore from the last *Walking Dead* episode he'd seen in order to make the damn thing wilt every time it stirred into action. His gaze slid to the door Jess had just gone through.

And with her around—her succulent mouth, her sly misty-gray eyes, her lush breasts and mouthwatering ass—he'd spent more time thinking about putting a screwdriver through a zombie's eye than his job, which was a whole other problem.

But between the friggin' honeymoon suite—a room designed exclusively for sex, for God's sake—the baby-making music in the elevator, the horny teenagers rubbing all over each other, that huge-ass bed and the porn...

He'd just about reached the end of his rope.

And to think that he'd thought this trip was going to be simple. Easy, even.

He smothered a laugh, then pushed away from the shower glass and shoved an unsteady hand through his hair, scouring the lowest part of his soul for the last bit of his willpower. He needed to focus on something besides the thought of Jess's lovely mouth sucking him dry. Honestly, if he didn't know better, he'd be certain that someone was screwing with him, testing him, setting him up.

Ridiculous, he knew. He was just looking for an excuse, someone to blame—other than himself—for completely losing focus. But he'd never been one to pass the buck or shirk his responsibilities, and he damn sure wasn't going to start now.

He was, however, going to call Payne.

"I was hoping you'd call," Payne said by way of greeting. "I'm assuming you've made it to the hotel without incident?"

"We have," Griff confirmed. "We've only just arrived in our room, but I've been through it and am confident that it's not going to be easily breached. It also offers the best escape route, should we need to flee."

Located on the northeast corner of the building, the sixteenth floor connected to the second tower of the hotel and provided a rapid service elevator to the kitchen, which opened into the parking garage. Though he hadn't timed it yet, he was certain they could be out of the hotel and into the SUV in less than two minutes, should the occasion arise.

"And the suite?" Payne asked. "I know it's not ideal, but I was assured there was a comfortable couch you could sleep on."

"I'm not here to be comfortable," Griff told him, which was a damn good thing since he was as friggin' uncomfortable as he could possibly get. "This is an ideal location and was the best choice for our purposes."

"And Ms. Rossi? How's she holding up?"

Griff felt a grin turn his lips. "She's fine," he said. "Doesn't seem the least bit worried."

Which was as flattering as it was concerning. He had absolutely no intention of letting the Owl steal her father's work, but he sincerely hoped her unwavering faith in his ability wasn't misplaced. This wasn't just any old ordinary thief after any old ordinary bra. This was a notorious professional who'd lifted items worth a whole helluva lot more than this two-and-a-half-million-dollar bra.

Regardless, the guy would have to pry it out of Griff's cold dead hands before he'd let him take it.

"Excellent," Payne said. "Per your request, I've arranged to have the handcuffs delivered. They should be there in the next few minutes."

"Good," Griff told him. "I want to go over every inch of this hotel and I'm not comfortable leaving the case in the in-room safe unless I'm in here, as well."

"Good call," Payne said. "It would be child's play for Keller."

Griff sidled over and leaned against the bathroom counter. "You knew him well then?" he asked, more than a little curious about the relationship between his straight-arrow boss and the notorious thief and forger. Talk about strange bedfellows.

Payne hesitated. "I don't know if anyone has ever or will ever know Keller well," he said. "But, out of our set at school, I think I knew him better than anyone else. His father was a real bastard. The old man routinely beat the shit out of him and, based on little things that he said then and I've had time to reflect on now, I think the abuse went further than anyone suspected. I've been looking at some of his earlier thefts and noticed a connection, one that I'm not sure many other people would be in the position to see. One that I'm not even sure is significant, but…"

"Oh?"

"Each one of those paintings, at one point or another, was part of his father's private collection."

Griff frowned in confusion. "So he stole them from his father?"

"No, that's just it. They weren't in his father's collection when they were stolen. They'd been sold or traded off."

"So why would he want them then? If he and his father had such a contentious relationship?"

Payne's sigh echoed over the line. "That's the million-dollar question, Griff. I don't know. I don't know that we'll ever know. But I do know this. Keller Thompson doesn't do anything without thorough cause and consideration. He would have evaluated every potential outcome and scenario before making the first move. And money isn't the motivator here—he inherited a sizable fortune when his father died. He's brilliant, he's charming, he's a natural leader." He chuckled. "Hell, even his targets like him."

"Do you? Still?"

"I do," Payne said without the slightest hesitation.

"Even though he's a thief?"

"Yes," he said. "Shocking, isn't it? I don't approve of what he does, but after you've spent six years in a dorm room with someone, you either love them or hate them. Keller and a select few others made that hellhole bearable for me. That kindness isn't easily dismissed."

Griff knew exactly what he was talking about because it was the same with war. There'd been several times he'd gone into situations with soldiers not of his choosing and had come away with a different perspective. There was something about simply *surviving* that forged a bond, whether you actually wanted it or not.

"There's something else, too," Payne said. "Did you notice that this is the first so-called job he's taken on in more than a year?"

He *had* noticed that. He'd chalked it up to either disinterest or financial security, but considering Payne's comment about Keller's inheritance, that was a moot point. He said as much. "What's your take on it?"

"I think he's come out of retirement," Payne said. "The best I've been able to tell, he's been spending the bulk of his time at his place on Little Kennesaw Mountain."

"Right on our front doorstep," Griff said, an odd feeling swirling in his gut. "Is he from Georgia?"

"No, he's from North Carolina, but he sold the family estate right after his father died. He lost his mother when he was seven. Car wreck. That's when his father had reluctantly taken him in. And then promptly moved him out," he added grimly.

Yes, it was sad and he couldn't help but feel a bit of regret for Keller's circumstances, but this history lesson didn't have a damn thing to do with their case. "Why would he come out of retirement?" Griff asked.

"Your guess is as good as mine," Payne told him. "But if he's done it to steal the Clandestine bra, I can assure you there's a good reason."

Griff's irritation spiked. "Not good enough," he said, unable to keep the low growl from his voice. "Can you get Charlie to research the registered guests in the hotel, particularly those on the fifteenth, sixteenth and seventeenth floors? I'd like her to flag every man from twenty-five to forty and forward me their room numbers." He'd already committed Keller's face to memory from the pictures Payne had forwarded. If he was in the hotel, he felt certain that he'd recognize him.

"I'll do it."

"I'm also going to need a master key," he said.

"Beau Morton is head of security for the hotel and he's aware of our circumstances. I'm sure he'd be able to help you with that."

"I'll look him up, thanks."

Payne hesitated again. "Listen, Griff, not that we doubt your capabilities, but we've been talking strategy here on our end and we're all of the opinion that the bra is most vulnerable when it's on the model, from the instant it goes on her body, onto the catwalk, then back offstage."

Yes, he'd mentioned that before and Griff was in total agreement, because it was the only time the damn thing would ever be off his wrist.

There was another pregnant pause. "Because of this, we think it would be best if the bra never went onto the model."

Griff blinked. Never went onto the model? But— "I don't see that scenario flying with any party involved here, Payne, least of all Jess." *Shit.* "Er, Ms. Rossi," he corrected.

"We can pull rank," Payne said. "It's in our contract. Ranger Security isn't going to handle anything worth two and a half million dollars and *not* have total authority on protecting the cargo."

Griff rubbed his eyes, wearily anticipating the riot he was going to have on his hands. No one was going to like this. Not Jess. Not Clandestine. Not Montwheeler. They were all going to be justifiably livid. And he was the lucky bastard who was going to get to break the news to them.

"Are you suggesting that we abort?" he asked. "That I return to Shadow's Gap?"

"That's not at all what I'm suggesting," Payne assured him. "What I'm suggesting is an amendment to the plan."

He wasn't certain he liked the direction this was going. "What kind of amendment?"

"We think it would be best if Ms. Rossi modeled the bra, with you as her escort."

Griff laughed nervously, certain that he had misunderstood. "Come again?"

"Think about it, Griff," Payne said. "The piece is at its most vulnerable when it leaves your wrist—when it goes into someone else's hands, onto the model. If it goes from your wrist directly onto Ms. Rossi, whom we're certain hasn't been compromised in any way, and you stay at her side from beginning to end, then we have a much better shot at thwarting Keller. His easiest 'in' on this job is through one of the models. I'm sure he's already recruited an unwitting accomplice."

He suspected Payne was right on all counts. Still… "And what if I can't get Ms. Rossi to agree?"

"She'll agree," he said. "Her father has put too much work into the piece for her to refuse."

There was that. She'd abandoned her own plans for the weekend to see this through for him. She knew what backing out altogether would mean for all parties involved. Payne was right. She would do it, in the end.

But not without a very vehement, prolonged and indignant resistance.

"Bring them all up to speed, but make sure that they keep the change of plans to themselves," Payne continued. "Changing the strategy is moot if Keller gets wind of it."

"All right," Griff told him. "I'll see to it."

But, *damn,* how he dreaded it.

8

HE WANTED HER to *what?* Stunned, Jess felt her eyes bug and her jaw drop. "Not no, but *hell,* no," she said, shaking her head. "I agreed to come as a family representative, not to actually put the damn thing on and walk out in front of a roomful of people." And the most notoriously critical people in the world, at that. Nausea curdled in her stomach and her mouth went bone dry at the mere idea.

There was no freakin' way.

"I understand your hesitation, Jess, but—"

She snorted. "You do, do you? You understand what it would be like to basically bare your own family jewels to what will eventually amount to *millions* of people?"

"I'll be right there with you," he said, taking a step closer to her. "I'm going to accompany you from one end of the runway to the other."

She arched an imperious brow. "In your underwear?"

He blinked, then swallowed. "Well, no, but—"

She shook her head again, cutting him off. "Then you don't know what the hell you're asking."

"And you don't seem to realize that I'm not *asking*," he said, his voice infused with a hint of steel. "I'm telling you that this is the only way we're moving forward."

She sucked in a breath, her gaze swinging to meet his again. "You can't be serious."

"I'm completely serious," he said levelly, an implacable glint in his eyes. "This was not the original plan, I know, but it's my job to work with the facts as I know them, in the framework that I've been given. *This* is the new reality. It's too dangerous to put the bra on anyone else. How do we know that the Owl hasn't already recruited one of the models? Perhaps the *very* model?"

She stilled. He had a point, but—

"The only thing that we know for sure is that an accomplished thief with a flair for the dramatic wants to take the bra." He stepped forward once more, his gaze lasering into hers. "What better time to snatch it than *during* the show?"

"What?" she asked incredulously. "You think he's going to swoop in like Tarzan, pop the snap and swing away with it?"

"Are you so certain that he couldn't?"

Not after reading everything about him, no, she wasn't. Jess dropped heavily onto the small sofa, hung her head and shoved her hands into her hair. "Why can't you just accompany the Clandestine model?" she asked. "Why does it have to be me?"

"Because I don't trust anyone but you," he said, surprising the hell out of her.

She glanced up, caught his equally astonished expression before he smoothed it away. She opened her mouth, shut it, then opened it again. "Well," she finally managed to say, "be that as it may, you're forgetting one important detail."

His brow furrowed with suspicion. "What is that?"

"It doesn't fit me."

Confusion cluttered his brow. "I'm sorry?"

"The bra," she said impatiently. "It was designed for a much smaller woman. One with a nonexistent rib cage and less—" she gestured awkwardly to her breasts "—junk in the cup," she improvised.

He stared at her chest, his blue-green gaze momentarily glazing over, his pupils dilating with desire. He looked like a starving man who'd just been given a ticket to an all-you-can-eat buffet. Her nipples tingled in response and an answering zing echoed in the heart of her sex. And he was just looking at her. Not touching her, not licking her, not...

He cleared his throat and with effort dragged his eyes from her breasts to her face. "I'm sure that something c-can be done t-to accommodate you."

"I don't want to be accommodated," she said desperately. "I want to keep my clothes on!"

His sympathetic but resolved gaze tangled with hers. "I'll give you a minute to make a decision," he said. "You are aware of the options."

Case securely clasped to his wrist with the handcuffs that arrived only moments ago, Griff turned and walked out of the living room and into the kitchen, presumably to get a drink while she decided whether to ruin her father and their business, or cram her girls into a bra that was two cup sizes too small and sacrifice her modesty on a group of people who would, if they were feeling generous, call her a cow. She had a minimum of thirty pounds on those Clandestine models. The idea of walking out there, practically naked, with every single eye trained on her breasts, made her want to vomit.

Violently.

Granted, Griff's hot lingering gaze inspired a different feeling in her altogether—he made her feel attractive, sexy, desirable—but that's because he was a man and men loved breasts. She rolled her eyes, smothered a whimper. But women? Women were vicious. Women judged.

But how could she refuse, really? She imagined trying to call her father and share the news, tell him that the past six months of his life's work was for nothing because she didn't like the idea of wearing the bra for five minutes. She'd rather be called fat a thousand times over in every language known to man than to do that to him. He was her dad, her only living parent. Her family. She swallowed, heard the clink of ice into a glass as Griff made himself a drink.

She sighed, lolled her head back onto the couch and closed her eyes as the reality of her immediate future settled on her shoulders. Geez, she could use a drink, as well. Something strong. Like vodka. Or rum. Or good old-fashioned whiskey.

"Well?" he said.

She hadn't heard him approach, which was hardly surprising. For such a big man he made very little noise. She cracked one eye open and looked at him. "I'm still thinking," she lied.

"Think faster."

She scowled at him. "Don't tell me you've already got a new schedule lined out."

He smiled and handed her a drink. "I've always got a schedule lined out."

"What is this?" she asked, peering into the glass.

"It's lime soda."

"Does it have a liberal dose of alcohol in it?"

He chuckled softly, the sound warm and strangely intimate. "No, why? Did you want it to?"

She made a moue of regret. "Would have been nice," she said. She looked up at him, noted the angle of his jaw, the sleek line of his brow, the purely sexy curve of his mouth, and released a breath. "I'll definitely need one tomorrow," she said, feeling her stomach quake with anxiety. "Before I make my modeling debut."

His gaze sharpened, then lit with admiration. "So you'll do it?"

"I will," she said, heartened by his approval. She suspected it took a lot to impress Griffin Wicklow. "Dad would be heartbroken if I didn't see this through," she continued. "He's put so much into it, has worked harder on this than anything else he's ever done." She smiled wanly. "He's convinced that it's going to fill the family coffers and make Rossi Jewelry a household name."

He watched her, the weight of his regard a near-physical thing. "And you? Do you think it will do that?"

She plucked a strawberry from the plate and took a bite. "Based on the upswing of orders we've seen since we were chosen to create the design, yes," she said, nodding. "I do."

"And is that what you want?"

No one, including her father, had ever asked her that, had ever asked her if she wanted the company to expand to the degree that this sort of exposure would generate. Her brother and sister, who didn't have anything to do with the business, had been overjoyed, and her father had been so swept up in the "Rossi legacy" that he'd neglected to factor in the way that this was going to change things. They'd have to hire more help, outsource the castings to meet demand, travel more, work more.

More, more, more.

No, it wasn't what she'd wanted. She'd wanted to continue their boutique, exclusive designs—create what she wanted, at her leisure, preferably from the comfort of her own home—and work on cars and race. It would all change now, she realized. Especially once she—a Rossi—modeled the piece.

"It's what he wants," she finally said, indirectly answering his question. "And that's what's important."

"What you want should be important, too."

While she appreciated the sentiment—admittedly, it was nice to have someone on "her team," so to speak—he was the last person who should be lecturing her about self-sacrifice.

Because he was the unquestionable king of it.

"You're one to talk," she said, careful to keep her tone light. "You gave up your career—your whole way of life—before even letting your sister see if she was a match for Justin."

It was a wonderful, wonderful thing. Purely selfless. Noble. The most honorable thing she'd ever heard of anyone doing for another person. She hadn't been lying when she'd said he was extraordinary. Because he was. And the kicker? The thing that genuinely, truly set him apart from everyone else?

He didn't know it. He didn't know how *good* he was. How much character he had.

In a world where personal responsibility was thin on the ground and entitlement the current battle cry of the masses, society desperately needed men like Griff. Men who were willing to step up and make the hard decisions. And from what she could tell, he'd been doing it since his father walked out all those years ago. Her heart ached for the boy who'd been lost, the one who'd had to become a man much earlier than time ordinarily dictated.

"That's different," he said, the smallest hint of shock registering on his achingly handsome face.

"Oh, really? How so?"

He shifted uncomfortably, then looked away. "It was surgery," he said, as though that explained everything. "I wasn't going to let her go through that when *I* was a match, when *I* could do it."

"Let me ask you something, Griff. If Justin hadn't needed a kidney, would you still be in the military?"

"Who knows?" he said, lifting a shoulder.

He knew, she thought. He just didn't want to answer her. "Well, what else might you be doing?"

"I might not be doing anything," he said, his blue-green gaze pinning her to the couch, clearly not liking the direction this conversation had taken. "I might be injured or dead."

Her chest squeezed painfully at the very thought, but she recognized deflection when she saw it. "Okay, provided that Justin hadn't needed a kidney and you weren't injured or dead, would you still be in the military?"

He was quiet for a moment, a spark of something kindling in his gaze. Respect, maybe? Because she hadn't let him off the hook? Because she'd pressed when no else had? "Yes, I would," he finally admitted.

She smiled knowingly, having scored her point. "So you put your family's needs first, right? Just like I'm doing."

Faint humor lit his gaze, his lips curling into a rueful grin. "I guess that makes you extraordinary as well, then, doesn't it?"

Jess grinned and lifted a shoulder. "Beats the hell out of the alternative," she said.

"Oh? What's that?"

"A fool."

Another chuckle bubbled up his throat. "Trust me, Jess, you are nobody's fool."

He was wrong, she thought, watching him from beneath her lashes. She was a fool for him. Already. And they weren't even halfway through the weekend yet.

HAVING FINALLY CONVINCED Jess that her modeling the piece was the only way forward, Griff knew that he'd need to present the new plan to both the Clandestine and Montwheeler representatives, and had requested an immediate meeting. Given what both companies had invested in what he would forever think of as "the damn bra," he didn't anticipate any problems.

Jess had changed out of her traveling clothes and donned a black business suit and heels. Small ruby ladybugs glittered from her ears and she'd attached a matching brooch to her jacket. Admittedly, Griff knew very little about jewelry, but he liked the look of what she wore. It was classy but whimsical. It had come as no surprise that the design was hers, part of the If It Crawls collection her father had mentioned.

As they boarded the elevator, Marvin Gaye's "Let's Get It On" playing this time—what the hell was it with this music? Griff wondered—he felt compelled to reiterate the obvious. "They'll get on board. They don't have a choice."

She harrumphed and slid him a knowing little glance. "You never saw *The Devil Wears Prada,* did you?"

"No." He didn't see what that had to do with anything.

"They—as in 'they' the fashion industry—thought Anne Hathaway was fat. *Anne Hathaway!*" she repeated incredulously. "Compared to Anne Hathaway, I'm a sasquatch." She shook her head. "They're never going to agree to it."

A sasquatch? Griff thought, blinking repeatedly,

stunned at the comment. *Her?* Didn't she own a mirror? Didn't she know how lovely she was? How damn sexy? Was that why she'd been so reluctant to do this? he wondered, an odd tingling in his gut. Because she was afraid she wouldn't measure up? Because she thought she was, of all things, *fat?*

Good Lord...it boggled the mind.

His gaze drifted over her body—the very evidence to the contrary—lingering on her plump, ripe breasts, the small indentation of her waist, the generous curve of her hip... He hardened again as need hammered through him, singeing his veins, blistering through reason and logic. He could take her right here, Griff thought. Slide those black slacks down over her womanly hips, lift her up, put her back against the wall and absolutely fuck the living hell out of her.

That's what she did to him.

And she thought she was fat.

He had to unclench his teeth to speak. "First of all, you are *not* a sasquatch. Honestly, woman, I don't know what you see when you look in the mirror, but if it's a sasquatch, then you need to book an appointment with an optometrist immediately." He took a step closer and was momentarily distracted by her mouth. "Second, I don't give a damn what *they* say, you are—" perfect, glorious, amazing, *mine,* he thought as she stared up at him, wide-eyed and a little shocked at his admittedly vehement reaction "—beautiful," he finally finished.

Her gaze held his for what felt like an eternity, then dropped to his mouth. She moistened her lips, her pale pink tongue sliding along the lower. "Th-thank you," she breathed unsteadily, leaning closer to him.

His heart pounded in his chest, the breath stuck in his lungs. He could smell her perfume—rose oil, he'd learned earlier—and could discern a tiny freckle just to the left of her right eye. To hell with it, Griff thought, going off book, off plan, as he lowered his head, her breath close enough to taste.

A mere nanosecond before his lips could touch hers, the elevator dinged, and they stilled, momentarily frozen in the moment. Griff smiled regretfully and carefully—reluctantly—withdrew.

The same couple who'd ridden up with them earlier walked in, laughing and holding hands, oblivious to what they'd just interrupted.

"Listen to that," the guy said, his smile significant and wide. "It's Marvin," he told his girlfriend, wrapping his hands around her waist, dragging her in for another especially loud kiss.

"Baby-making music," the girl responded with a low giggle. "This elevator definitely has the best tunes. We should wait for this one every time, eh, Marcus?" She laughed again. "I wonder if it takes requests?" she asked, looking up, presumably for a speaker or hidden camera. "How about a little Barry White next time?"

"How about staying in their room?" Jess leaned over and whispered low into his ear. "Honestly," she added with an eye roll.

Griff grinned. "I'm bringing a water bottle with me next time," he said. "We'll spray 'em. Like a cat."

She shook with laughter, bit her lip, and something

about that grin punched him right in the gut, leaving him oddly shaken and breathless. He swallowed. "I'm sorry about this," he said, gesturing to the case in his hand. "I wish there was another way."

Regardless of how misguided or unfounded—how mystifying—her insecurities were real in her own head and it took an admirable amount of courage to set them aside for someone else. He inwardly smiled. Of course, only an idiot would take Jess Rossi for a coward and Griff was many things, but an idiot wasn't one of them.

"It's not your fault," she told him, her gaze warm, her lids sweeping to half-mast. "And despite my…reaction, I know that you're right and—" she lifted her shoulders in a helpless little shrug "—I trust you."

I trust you. Three simple words. A wealth of meaning. And with that sentiment resounding in his head, they exited the elevator and made their way to the private room where the others were waiting. After showing them the piece and the subsequent oohing and aahing subsided, Griff quickly brought the group up to speed, efficiently laying out the facts, and presented the new plan.

Shocked silence thundered through the room.

"It's out of the question," the CEO of Clandestine announced after a long moment. His gaze swung to Jess's. "No offense to Ms. Rossi," he quickly added. "But this is our biggest show of the year. We've invested a lot of time and money into this event, and we have an image to protect. Our models are selected based on that image and…" He hesitated, shifted uncomfortably.

"And Ms. Rossi doesn't fit that image," his second-in-command, a reed-thin, tight-faced fortysomething woman whose eyebrows didn't move finished.

Jess shot him an arch look, smiled knowingly.

"Evidently, I didn't make myself clear, Ms....?" Griff looked at the frozen woman and arched a deliberate brow.

"Angelique Blaylock," she finished haughtily, her nostrils thinning as though conversation with him was a tedious waste of her time.

"Blaylock," he repeated. "This issue is not up for debate. My company was hired to protect Montwheeler's investment. And, per the contract you signed with Montwheeler, and each of you, in turn, signed with Ranger Security, I am the final authority on the matter. In light of the imminent threat against the piece, this is the only way I'm willing to proceed. Ms. Rossi will model, I will escort her. The alternative is to cancel the show."

She gasped. "But that's not possible! It's too late! You have no idea what you're suggesting!"

"Yes, I do, Ms. Blaylock and, like Ms. Rossi here," he said, nodding at her, "I suggest you adjust and make the best of it."

"I agree," the Montwheeler representative, Harold Pershing, said with a decisive nod. He looked a bit different from the picture Griff had been given—thinner maybe?—but photographs weren't always completely accurate. "No one here has as much to lose as we do and, considering the significant threat against our investment, I believe it's the wisest course of action with the least amount of liability for all parties."

Ms. Blaylock turned and sneered at him, her eyes burning with condescension. "You don't know what you're talking about! You know nothing of fashion!"

He merely smiled. "Probably not, but I have a keen grasp on value and I know what my gems are worth." He glanced at Jess. "And Ms. Rossi knows how much work went into making the piece, which is no doubt why she's agreed to do this." He shot a look at Mr. Nolan and Ms. Blaylock, and lifted a brow. "If I were you, I'd be thanking Ms. Rossi for her willingness to save the day, and complimenting Mr. Wicklow on his ingenuity and resourcefulness. I, for one, am very grateful."

Griff watched Jess nod her thanks, her tense expression wilting with a bit of relief.

"It's not that we're ungrateful," Mr. Nolan remarked. "We are," he insisted. "But we've got a contract with the model, as well." His expression went slack. "Sahara is not going to be pleased."

"With all due respect, Mr. Nolan, that's not my problem," Griff told him.

Ms. Blaylock had been eyeing Jess with a speculative gleam, her waxy, unnaturally puffy lips pursed. "The hair is workable, bone structure is nice. Smile," she commanded, to which Jess obliged more out of surprise than obedience, Griff imagined. "She'll need bleaching." Her gaze slid down the rest Jess's body, as if she was a horse the representative was considering purchasing, and then she grimaced and shook her head. "There aren't enough laxatives and diuretics in the world to get you down to size by tomorrow, but a detox wrap will shave a few inches off and every little bit will help. We've never used a plus-size model before," she said to Nolan. "It could be good for PR." She glanced at Jess once more. "Have you eaten already?"

Seemingly distracted, it took her a second to respond. "I've had breakfast, but not lunch."

Another wince. "No more food. Juice only. Until after the show. Beyond that, you can gorge all you want to," she said, her nose wrinkling with distaste.

Having reached the end of her patience, Jess's eyes rounded. "I don't gorge. I *eat*. Because it's *healthy*."

"Whatever." The woman picked up her cell phone and looked at Mr. Nolan. "I've got to warn Andre," she said. "Let him know he's got his work cut out for him."

Griff frowned. "Who is Andre?"

"Our stylist," she answered without looking at him. "Or in this case, our magician," she added snidely, casting a significant look in Jess's direction.

Though he'd always prided himself on being level-headed, on making decisions based on data and logic, not on emotion, Griff suddenly saw red. A haze of anger so intense it made his fingers shake descended over him and, while his voice was low, it still cracked like lightning through the room when he spoke.

"Enough," he said, gratifyingly making Ms. Blaylock jump. He stared a hole through her, so furious he could barely breathe. "Ms. Rossi will not be modeling the bra after all, because it isn't going to make its much anticipated appearance." He straightened. "We're leaving."

Jess's mouth dropped open. "Griff, no," she said, shaking her head.

"What?" Ms. Blaylock gasped. "But you can't be serious— You can't mean—"

Griff bared his teeth at her. "Oh, but I do," he snarled. "Because Ms. Rossi is under my protection, as well," he said in a clipped tone. "And do you know what that means, Ms. Blaylock? That means that I'm not going to permit her to be insulted and abused, especially from an employee of the very company she's so graciously offered to help."

"Griff, really, you don't have to—"

He whirled on her. "Yes, I do," he insisted. "I'm not going to let her talk to you like that. You're *amazing*," he said. "You're clever and interesting and fearless and *good,* dammit, which makes you so much more attractive than anyone else they could ask to do this." He smiled at her. "The icing on the cake is that you're heart-stoppingly *gorgeous,"* he continued. "Stunning, perfect and so damn sexy I've been—" He stopped, then frowned and shook his head. "Never mind what I've been, that's not the point. The point is that there isn't a single heterosexual man alive who could look at you and find you wanting." He released a long breath. "You're *smokin'* hot and I'm not going to let her or anyone else," he added darkly, "tell you otherwise. Understood?"

She stared at him, her misty-gray eyes lighting with

pleasure and something else, something he couldn't quite identify, then she smiled, almost shyly, and nodded. "Understood."

He helped her with her chair, then propelled her to the door.

"Wait! Please!" Mr. Nolan and Mr. Pershing both objected simultaneously.

Griff paused, his pulse still thundering in his ears, and shot a look over his shoulder. "I'm sorry, gentlemen."

"But there has to be something we can do," Mr. Nolan implored. "Please reconsider. Ms. Rossi, I am so sorry for my colleague's behavior. Mr. Wicklow is quite right. You're a lovely woman and very—" Mopping his sweating brow, he struggled to find the right word. And he certainly wasn't going to find the right one written on her breasts, Griff thought darkly, which was precisely where he was looking.

"Desirable," Mr. Pershing finished.

"Yes!" Mr. Nolan agreed with obvious relief. "Desirable. What will it take to make you stay?" he asked. "Name it and it's yours. Anything."

Griff's hard gaze slid to Ms. Blaylock. "She leaves now and doesn't come back until we're gone."

"What? No!" she said scoffingly. "Don't be ridiculous. It's my show."

Mr. Nolan turned to look at her, his face grim. "Not anymore, Angelique. Clarice will take over from here."

She growled, enraged, and threw her water glass against the wall.

"All right, then," Griff said, pleased. "Have Clarice

send me a schedule." And with that parting comment, he smiled and opened the door, leaving them to deal with an outraged but thoroughly demoted Ms. Blaylock.

Booyah.

9

HEART HAMMERING IN her ears, hands shaking, Jess walked quietly beside Griff back to the elevator. She'd never imagined that a person could be stunned senseless from happiness, but she was living, shallowly breathing proof of it.

No one had ever—*ever*—stood up for her like that.

Having been a bit of an oddity growing up, there'd been plenty of sarcasm and teasing sent her way—most of it from boys she'd bested at something—and even the guys who she'd ultimately counted as friends had never fully had her back, the supposition being that she didn't need anyone to be her champion, that she could slay her own dragons.

And she could. In fact, she had so often that it was second nature now. She'd never expected anyone to do it for her.

The only thing that had kept her from diving across the table and slapping the hell out of that sanctimonious bitch's surgically altered, condescending face was the image of her father, his weary head bent over the bra as he painstakingly set the jewels. Though admittedly it was making her miserable, she'd been willing to bear the insults and ridicule for him.

Then that Blaylock woman had uttered that "magician" comment and Jess had watched a thundercloud of anger descend over Griff's achingly handsome face. His eyes had flashed, then narrowed, his mouth virtually vanished into a thin hard line and his face had set so quickly it had almost appeared frozen.

He'd been willing to abort his first mission—to call everything off and put his reputation on the line—*for her.*

And if that hadn't been enough to merit a float-worthy moment—when joy had practically lifted her feet off the ground—then his impassioned declaration of all her finer points, which had begun with character traits and ended with physical attributes, certainly had been.

You're amazing, clever, interesting, fearless— which, strictly speaking, wasn't true because she'd told him about the clowns—*and good.*

Then *gorgeous* and *sexy.*

Not only were his impassioned compliments the nicest things anyone had ever said about her, he'd gotten them in the right order, by the characteristics that were the most important to her.

Evidently her silence had stretched too long because Griff sent her a cautious look as the elevator doors opened. He held it for her, allowing her to precede him into the small space, then depressed the floor number.

Impossibly, Barry White's smooth, low voice echoed around them.

"Listen," he said, turning to face her. "Before you clobber me for not letting you handle that yourself, I just want you—"

"Would it be all right if I kissed you?" She didn't know what made her stop and ask first, when they'd been so close to doing that very thing in this same elevator less than half an hour ago, but for reasons that escaped her, it seemed important. Necessary, even.

Evidently shocked, a flare of heat so intense it nearly sucked the air out of her lungs sparked in his gaze, deepened the blue, electrified the green.

He swallowed. "You want to kiss me?" he asked, his voice low and hoarse.

Jess nodded, took a step toward him, close enough to see how his lashes tangled at the ends, to smell his cologne, something warm and spicy with an understated musky finish. She deliberately let her gaze drop to his mouth, could feel her heart thundering in her chest as longing hammered steadily through her.

"Desperately," she admitted baldly.

The very corners of his purely carnal lips curled into the faintest, sexiest, most satisfied grin she'd ever seen. It was all the answer Jess needed and, anticipation making her belly quiver, she fisted his shirt in her hands, rose on tiptoe and pressed her lips against his.

Fiery gooseflesh raced from the tips of her toes to the top of her head, making every hair on her body rise to attention, then backtracked and settled at the base of her spine. Warmth mushroomed from her shivery womb, blanketing her sex in an achy, needy heat that almost made her whimper in response.

His lips were soft but firm, and they moved over hers slowly at first, as though he wanted to savor the taste of her, absorb the sensation of her mouth beneath his. She could feel the tension vibrating through him, knew that the dam of his desire was creaking and groaning, ready to give way, and yet he held firm, seemingly determined not to rush the first meeting of their mouths— their very first kiss—and Jess found herself equally touched and irritated.

She didn't want him to hold back.

She wanted him to lose that tightfisted control, to deviate from his damn schedule, to forget the rules and protocol and think only of her. Selfish? Yes. Stupid? Possibly. Did she care?

Hell, no.

Releasing his shirt, she slipped her hands up over his broad shoulders and around his neck into his hair, pressing herself more firmly against him. As though she'd tripped some sort of secret trigger, he released a low, thrilling growl, lashed his arm around her waist, drawing her closer, and slid his tongue into her mouth. Though she would have thought it impossible to freeze and melt simultaneously, that's exactly what happened to her. Every muscle in her body responded, quaking with anticipation, melting with need.

She rubbed her thumb along the soft skin behind his ear, cupped his cheek with her hand and fed at his mouth, the kiss deep and drugging, the expert stroke of his tongue as it tangled around hers the perfect complement to the delicious drag and pull of his lips against her own.

And, *man,* could he kiss.

He knew when to be soft, when to be firm, when to slide and when to suckle, used his tongue as a tool of pleasure, not a dagger to stab into her mouth, and he'd mastered the moisture ratio, having hit the mystical sweet spot between too dry and too sloppy.

More significant, her panties were damp and he hadn't even gotten to second base yet.

Jess dimly noted the tinkling of a bell, but the small cough and chuckle that followed it, much to her mortification, registered. She and Griff abruptly sprang apart as a new passenger entered the elevator, but he held on to her hand, his strong fingers threading through hers, and there was something even more intimate in the seemingly innocuous gesture than the kiss they'd just shared. Inexplicable delight bloomed in her chest, along with the faintest ring of warning, which she purposely ignored.

"Oh, please don't stop on my account," the newcomer drawled, his dark brown eyes crinkling with humor at the corners. "Love makes the world go round, eh?"

His voice was a little too high and dramatic for a man and a smudge of eyeliner blurred beneath his lower lashes. His dark blond hair had been liberally streaked with platinum and gelled into a sculpture rather than an actual style. He wore black leather pants, a royal-blue shirt with a satin sheen and more jewelry than Johnny Depp. He held a large beat-up attaché in one hand and a cell phone in the other, which he perused with a negligent grin as he lounged against the wall.

He laughed delightedly at something on the screen, then held it up so that they could see. "Aw, would you look at my baby," he said. "Isn't she the cutest thing you've ever seen?"

His "baby" was a tiny Yorkie with an even tinier pink bow between its pert little ears. The adorable animal was in the arms of a smiling, heavily muscled man with extremely groomed eyebrows, his lightly glossed lips puckered into a blow kiss.

Jess highly suspected the guy in the photo was their fellow passenger's baby, as well.

Griff smiled and grunted noncommittally. Jess nodded. "Very sweet."

He grinned, seemingly pleased. "We shamelessly spoil the little bitch," he confided. "Regular walks, organic food, gourmet treats, and she's got her own pillow on our bed, but that's usually the way it works, right?" He heaved a small sigh, looked at the picture once more. "We don't own our pets, they own us."

Jess agreed, then nodded a goodbye at the man when they exited the elevator, her hand still in Griff's.

"He was certainly a character," she remarked.

Griff merely smiled. "That's one way of putting it."

"Oh? What would be your way?"

His eyes dropped to her mouth, flared with hunger. "I'm pretty sure you were looking at your stylist, the infamous Andre."

"Really. Wow." She nodded, not exactly sure what to make of that information. "All righty then."

"You know what else he was?" Griff asked her.

"No, what?"

"An unwanted interruption," he said. "You weren't finished kissing me yet."

Jess bit her lip as a thrill whipped through her. She'd been mildly worried that the dog lover in the elevator might have been a welcome distraction for Griff, one to give him the necessary wherewithal to resist her again.

She did *not* want him to resist. She wanted him to make her a part of his plans, to map out a schedule of seduction so depraved and thorough and wicked that they made every use of every amenity in their suite.

Starting with, but not limited to, the bed.

Careful to scan their surroundings, Griff approached the door and released her hand long enough to withdraw the key card and insert it into the lock. He bolted the door, throwing the additional lock he'd personally installed earlier, then made his usual sweep of the suite, checking for any hint of disturbance or anomaly.

He glanced at the coffee table and frowned. "Did you eat a second strawberry?" he asked.

Jess hesitated. "I'm not sure. Why?"

"There's one missing."

Wow. She knew that he was keeping a vigilant eye on everything, but to notice an extra strawberry was missing from the plate? She considered the question once more, then winced. "I think I did, actually," she said. "Right before we went downstairs."

He nodded, seemingly satisfied, then untucked his shirt and lifted it, revealing those glorious abs again, the taut line of coppery masculine hair below his navel, and pulled a strip of surgical tape from his side. He held it up for her perusal, indicating the pair of small keys stuck to the back.

"A pocket is too risky," he explained.

She smiled, impressed by his ingenuity. "That's clever."

To her surprise, he pulled a gun from the back of his waistband—she'd assumed he had one, but seeing it was another matter altogether—and then removed the cuff from his wrist and stored the case in the in-room safe in the bedroom. He hadn't done that before, so she could only assume that he was confident that the box was secure enough to take the risk. She watched him hide the keys beneath a block of smoked cheddar cheese in the refrigerator—inspired, she had to admit—and then he turned and, smiling lazily, sauntered toward her. It was a purposeful but unhurried gait that she found instantly arousing—a damn-near swagger, for lack of a better term—and his grin was endearingly boyish, but hot and promised sin.

A shaky breath leaked out of her lungs as he paused before her, his heavy-lidded gaze searching hers. He reached up and framed her face with the rim of his palms, the pad of his fingers warm against her skin. He slid his thumb along her jaw, eliciting a shiver. "The case was in the way," he murmured. "I'm going to need both hands for this."

Ah, Jess thought as giddy expectation bolted through her. So he *did* have a plan.

GRIFF DIDN'T SO much have a plan as a purpose and that purpose involved getting her naked as soon as possible and losing himself in the soft valley between her breasts and the even silkier heat between her thighs.

He'd fought the good fight. He'd lost.

But if this was losing, he thought as he tilted her face up to meet his and slanted his mouth over her sighing lips, then clearly being a winner was overrated.

Honestly, when she'd asked if she could kiss him, he'd been so shocked at the request, he'd had to lock his knees to keep from staggering. No one had ever *asked* for permission to kiss him—as if *she* was concerned about taking advantage of *him,* of all things—and that simple request from that sinfully beautiful mouth had shattered what had been left of his control.

Hell, it had been in shreds, anyway.

He'd never been more drawn to a woman, never been more fascinated or charmed, never wanted one with this sort of utterly relentless intensity, the kind that dogged his every footstep, haunted every thought, seeped into his very bones.

She had that effect on him. God help him, only *her*.

She was the infection and the cure, the disease and the antidote, the sickness and the remedy. His Achilles' heel. His Kryptonite.

His undoing.

Though he doubted Ranger Security would see it that way, he was—for the very first time in his life— going to ignore the consequences of his actions in favor of his own selfishness. If they had anything to say about it, he'd reference their own wives and tell them all to go to hell. He and Jess were consenting adults and what they got up to in the privacy of the hotel room the company was paying for was nobody's damn business.

THERE WAS A SIGNIFICANT flaw in that thinking, but he determinedly ignored it and drew her closer, deepening the kiss and stroking the sweet curve of her cheeks. She made a little sound, one that rang with desperation and pleasure, of need in its basest form, and his balls tightened in response, his cock thickening. A twitchy heat rushed through his veins as her hands pushed into his hair, massaging his scalp, and he gathered her against him, felt the weight of her lush, wonderful breasts against his chest.

"Bed," she murmured between kisses. "Now."

Griff smiled against her mouth, then without warning, he lifted her up, eliciting a little squeak of surprise from her throat. She accommodatingly wrapped her legs around his waist and, as he filled both hands with her wonderful heart-shaped rump, he felt another strike of heat land in his loins. The massive four-poster loomed large in the bedroom, a veritable oasis, and he followed her down onto the decadent softness, ate another sigh of pleasure from her ripe lips.

Seemingly desperate for the feel of him beneath her hands, she tugged at his shirt, pulling it fully from the waistband of his pants, then slid a greedy palm along his side, over his ribs. A low groan issued from her throat, one that, impossibly, made him even hotter.

Determined to feel her as well, Griff left her mouth and pressed a line of kisses along her jaw, down her throat while simultaneously slipping the front buttons of her shirt from their closures. Creamy skin, the swell of breasts above the lace edge of her bra, a nipple pushing through the silky fabric, pouting for him, ready for him.

He slid his nose down the middle of her chest, breathing her in, then traced the plump curve of her breast with his tongue before latching on to the crest and pulling it into his mouth through the fabric.

She inhaled sharply, mewled low, then squirmed against him even as her dextrous hand found the snap of his pants. He popped the front clasp of her bra to the tune of his own zipper whining, then bared her breasts with his teeth as her hand wrapped around him.

He closed his eyes tightly and shuddered from the intimate contact. Though a part of him longed to take things slow, to gradually discover her, to push her to the absolute brink before following her over, desire obliterated the sentiment, delivering a knockout punch to every inclination to dally.

There'd be time enough for that later.

Right now he just needed her. Needed to feel the rasp of his tongue against her nipples, her firm legs around his waist, her hot, wet heat surrounding him as he plunged dick deep into the welcoming cradle of her thighs. He wanted her hands on his ass, her mouth against his throat and his name screaming from her lips as he pounded into her, slaking the full measure of his lust in her glorious, womanly body.

Blessedly, she seemed to arrive at the same conclusion just as he did and she tore at his clothes, shoving his pants down his legs, then dragging his shirt over his head. Because being naked alone was as out of the question as unfair, Griff reciprocated in kind. Her slacks and panties got kicked to the foot of the bed and her jacket and shirt slung onto the floor, along with her bra.

He drew back to look at her, slipping his hands down over her sweet belly, the generous curve of her hip, and took in the thatch of silky mink curls at the top of her sex. Her breasts were mouthwateringly magnificent, full and crowned with dusky-pink nipples, puckered and waiting for his attention.

He released a shuddering breath as need and something else, not as easily defined and pretty damn terrifying, reached critical mass.

She reminded him of a Renaissance painting he'd once seen in Florence by the Italian master Titian— *Venus of Urbino.* She was sprawled across the down comforter, unapologetically feminine, blatantly sensual and unwittingly erotic. Her dark hair spilled out over the bed, her lovely mouth swollen from his kisses and her sleepy-looking dark gray gaze raked boldly over his body, lingering on his chest, his abdomen, his cock.

It, naturally, hardened further, practically preening beneath that sultry stare.

After what seemed like an eternity, her gaze bumped back into his and the slightest upturn of her lips beckoned with an unspoken invitation. Griff leaned forward and snagged a condom from the bedside drawer—this suite really was well equipped, he thought as he tore into the small foil package, withdrew the protection and quickly rolled it into place.

She glanced at his erection and snickered, which was, for obvious reasons, not the reaction a man wanted when a woman inspected his junk. "Leopard print? Really?"

Having been so distracted by the naked woman lying ready on the bed, Griff had not paused to inspect the protection he'd donned. He did now and felt his lips twitch. He glanced back at her and growled low, his own poor impersonation of the large cat, then determinedly crouched low and carefully sprang onto her, playfully biting her neck as he nudged her entrance.

"That was impressive," she said, laughing softly. She wrapped her arms around him, slid her nails down his back—not hard enough to break skin, but enough to get his attention. His skin prickled with gooseflesh. "Can you do other animals, as well?"

He drew back, laved her breast with his tongue, then pulled the tight bud into his mouth as he pushed into her. Her breath left her in a soundless *whoosh,* her muscles tightened around him and he squeezed his eyes shut as sensation blasted through him. His chest tightened, a fluttery heat winged through his belly and his cock felt as if it had died and gone to heaven. She was hot and tight and fit him like a glove, as though she'd been made expressly for him. And though they were only joined in the usual place, he felt the connection from one end of his body to the other—on a cellular level—and it was as exquisite as it was terrifying.

Because being afraid of anything, least of all sex,

was unacceptable, Griff batted the notion away and coupled his "mountain lion" impression with another ball-deep thrust. He desperately needed some humor to lighten the moment, to try to convince himself that these feelings weren't quite as significant as he suspected.

"Cougar," he panted, doing it again and again, thrusting harder and deeper, then deeper still. "Leopard, cheetah, lynx, jaguar."

She smiled and clung to him, drew her legs back, opening farther for him, then grabbed his ass and squeezed with desperate tension, clawing need in her frantic touch. She bent forward and licked his neck, a sleek path along the underside of his jaw, a sensitive area he hadn't known existed until she'd found it with her tongue.

Impossibly, he hardened more, could feel the tightening coil of climax circling in the back of his loins, and another low growl issued from his throat.

"What was that?" she asked.

He laughed, lifted her hips off the bed and plunged deeper. "Me," he said. "Just me."

"It was my favorite," she breathed brokenly, then tightened around him, fisted repeatedly, seemingly determined to make him lose it before she did.

Hell would freeze over first.

He reached between their joined bodies and massaged her clit, circling the engorged little kernel with the pad of his thumb. She sucked in a sharp breath, then swore hotly. "Dammit to hell— That's not— But you can't—"

Griff smiled down at her and increased the tempo. "I can't what?"

She glared at him, the muscles straining in her neck as she wrestled with the sensation. Her breath came in jagged little puffs, her glorious rosy-tipped breasts shook on her chest, absorbing each one of his frantic thrusts, and she clamped her feminine muscles around him once more, fisting tighter in an attempt to hold him, keep him there with her.

Harder, faster, deeper, he pistoned in and out of her, chasing after her release, determined to see her satisfied first, to see the exact moment when she lost it for him, when she came for him.

And it was worth it, Griff thought as every muscle in her body seized violently, bowing her back up off the bed, the hot greedy walls of her sweet sex bearing down on his aching cock. A silent scream ripped from her opened mouth and her cheeks blazed with color as she clung to him, held him, her shaking fingers biting into his flesh. Still convulsing around him, she leaned forward and licked his nipple, drew the small nub into her mouth and captured it lightly between her teeth.

The little shock of pleasurelike pain tore the breath out of his lungs and ripped release from the back of his balls. He shuddered violently as the orgasm tore through him, set his toes deep into the mattress and locked himself into her silky heat. His release triggered another aftershock of pleasure from her and she quaked anew, her breathing ragged and satisfied.

His limbs limp as noodles, Griff lifted himself off her, neatly disposed of the condom into the bedside trash, then hauled her firmly up against him. She made a low, contented sound and settled more comfortably into the wall of his chest.

"What was that?" he teased, referencing her own little noise.

She chuckled softly. "That was the sound of a satisfied woman," she said. "It's a little disturbing that you don't recognize it."

Pleasantly exhausted, Griff laughed and slung an arm over his forehead. "Maybe I just need to hear it a few more times. You know, so I can commit it to memory."

She turned and pressed a lingering kiss against his jaw, her twinkling, sated gaze tangling with his. "That sounds like a plan."

He grinned. "That's me, baby. The man with the plan."

And right now his only plan revolved around her, the bottle of massage oil he'd noticed in the drawer and a tiger-striped condom. Beyond that, who knew?

But he suspected Jessalyn Rossi was going to be a significant part of his future.

10

HOURS LATER, AFTER she'd attended several press events, met the much nicer Clarice and underwent a necessary but mortifying "fitting" for the bra, during which Griff naturally had to stand guard, Jess was mentally and physically exhausted. It wasn't that she minded him seeing her breasts—she rather liked the way he looked at them, actually, the way that hot hungry stare made her feel—but having him watch as Clarice and a seamstress literally adjusted her nipples for her and tsked over the removal of the push-up padding was more than a little awkward.

"I'm thrilled that you're doing this," the seamstress, Marjory, had told her. "It's a giant step forward if you ask me, having a normal-size model on the cover of the magazine. You'll be an inspiration to women everywhere."

Jess had merely smiled. She didn't know about that, but she appreciated the sentiment all the same. It had certainly beaten the hell out of Ms. Blaylock's opinion, that was for damn sure.

She mentally gave the hateful woman a single-finger salute, and happily took another bite of her cheeseburger. Griff sat next to her on the small sofa, his gaze roaming over more intel Ranger Security had provided. The soft glow of the fire cast a halo of coppery light around his head, illuminating his curls. He'd stripped off his shirt and pants, revealing gleaming skin over mouthwatering muscle, and lounged comfortably in his boxers, his long masculine feet kicked out in front of him. Aside from when they'd dozed this afternoon, it was the most relaxed she'd seen him. She loved the sleek turn of his bare shoulder, the exact spot where it met his neck. It made her hot. Hell, who was she kidding?

He made her hot.

He sent her a slant-eyed look, humor lighting his gaze. "You're staring."

She lifted one shoulder in a shrug and dragged a fry through a puddle of ketchup. "What do you expect? You're practically naked."

"You could be, too, if you wanted. You'd get no objection from me."

She'd just bet she wouldn't. She'd never felt more beautiful than she had this afternoon, when he'd been hovering above her, his big powerful body thrusting into hers while he raked her bare skin with his blistering gaze. Her lady bits quivered, remembering, and a hot rush of sensation tingled in her sex.

It had been unbelievably exquisite, the exact moment when he'd pushed inside her. She'd been breathless, shattered, rebuilt and reborn all in an instant. It was as though every minute leading up to that one had been for nothing—utterly pointless—and every moment going forward would be forever tied to it, as well.

It had been a significant turning point, she thought, but whether that would be for better or for worse remained to be seen. Though she'd love to explore this… *thing* between them—to see if the fiery connection could burn indefinitely or if, like a dying star, it would simply blaze magnificently for a little while and then fade away into insignificance—she wasn't sure it was such a good idea.

Aside from the fact that she didn't know whether Griff would even want to continue their—relationship? acquaintance? affair? whatever the appropriate label— beyond this weekend, the logistics alone would be a nightmare. Granted, other couples managed to make long-distance relationships work, but she imagined that there was an endgame plan, one that ultimately resulted in one or the other party relocating.

Unfortunately, that was out of the question for both of them.

Griff's job and family were in Atlanta. Her job and father were in Shadow's Gap. Neither scenario was likely to change, and it was a long damn way from Georgia to West Virginia.

Even if they wanted to try to make it work—and admittedly she was just smitten enough to be so inclined—chances were they'd only be setting themselves up for heartache later. Or, at the very least, she would.

Though she hadn't known Griff long enough to really know him—his likes and dislikes, foibles and fetishes—she still knew enough about him to recognize the key elements of his character, the kind of man he was, the kind of man he strived to be...and, frighteningly, that was enough for her to be half in love with him already.

Point of fact, she'd never been in love before and, while most of her friends were married and had children, Jess had never felt as though her life was lacking or unfulfilled because she didn't. She was happy with the status quo. Though she'd dated enough men who'd passed muster—who weren't intimidated by her hobbies or independence—she'd nevertheless never met one who made her want to don a veil and give up birth control. Were a husband and family of her own anywhere in her future? She didn't know. She supposed it could happen. But if it didn't, she'd never doubted that that would be all right, as well. She cast a covert glance at the man next to her.

But if there was ever a guy who could make her second-guess herself, then it was Griffin Wicklow.

She was playing with fire, Jess thought, dancing too damn close to the flames.

His cell vibrated on the coffee table, drawing her attention and, though she didn't intentionally read the display, she noticed it, anyway. Justin again. He seemed to text a lot, which described nearly every teenager in the modern world, she knew, but she couldn't help but wonder if there was more to it for Griff's little brother.

Her antennae had been twitching where the boy was concerned.

Griff casually leaned forward, picked up his phone and read the text. To the untrained eye, one might have thought his expression didn't change, but Jess perceived the slightest tightening around his mouth.

"What's wrong?"

Seemingly startled, his gaze swung to hers. "Nothing," he said. "It's just a text from Justin. He wants me to call him again."

"Oh, okay." She leaned forward, preparing to stand. "I'll give you some privacy then."

He grabbed her arm, tugged her back onto the couch. "I don't need any privacy," he told her. "I'm not going to call him back right now."

Something about the "right now" sounded off, as if he'd tacked the words onto the end of the sentence for her benefit. "Why not?" Jess asked. "We're finished for the evening. There are no more press events or fittings."

"You should have gone to dinner with Mr. Pershing and Mr. Nolan," he said, evidently trying to change the subject. He had diversion tactics down to an art form. "You didn't have to refuse on my account."

"I didn't," she lied. There was no way in hell she would have left him alone to guard the bra. Not that he wasn't fully capable of taking care of himself or that she expected to be a whole lot of help if they were attacked, but the idea of being away from him to deal with it on his own had been out of the question.

She strongly suspected he'd been left too much to deal with on his own.

He grinned at her, lifted a disbelieving brow. "You're telling me you'd rather have a room-service cheeseburger than a gourmet meal at one of the finest restaurants New York has to offer?"

"Truthfully, no," she admitted with a regretful shrug. "But the company is much better here."

His smile widened, evidence that he'd liked her response.

"You never answered my question," she reminded him.

His grin momentarily froze. "What question?"

Jess rolled her eyes. "Really? We're going to play this game again?" She heaved a disappointed sigh. "It would be so much more efficient if you'd just tell me what I want to know."

"Efficient?" he repeated, nearly gaping at her. "That's the word you've decided best communicates your nosiness?"

"Of course not," she said. "It's the one I thought would most appeal to you."

Impossibly, he looked even more shocked. He shook his head. "You're shameless, you know that?"

She nodded once. "I am. Now, what's the problem with calling your brother?" Family was family. She didn't buy into this "half" business. "Is he irritating? Annoying? Do you not like him? What?"

Griff sighed, looked away and passed a hand over his face. She could tell he was debating the merit of telling her to mind her own damn business versus confiding in her. She desperately hoped that he chose the latter.

He released another breath, then shot her a dark but resigned look. "No, he's not irritating or annoying," he said, much to her triumphant relief. "And yes, as it happens, I do like him." He looked away, staring at the fire. "He's a good kid."

Jess felt her brow furrow with confusion. "Then I don't understand. What's the problem?"

He dropped heavily back against the couch. "The problem is that he wants a relationship with me, and it's going to cause pain to other members of my family."

Ah. She inclined her head. "Your mom and sister would object?" While she wasn't in possession of all the facts and history, that seemed a little harsh. It wasn't Justin's fault that his father was an ass any more than it was anyone else's.

He shook his head. "No, they wouldn't—that would be petty," he added, then hesitated. "But my mother never got over my father and, while Glory never really knew him, I know that his absence hurt her. Justin is the kid my father raised, and his mother is the one my father didn't leave." He lifted a shoulder, his gaze haunted with helplessness. "Whether it's fair or not, Justin's a reminder of all that. I can't just ignore it because we share DNA."

Jess winced, offered a sympathetic smile. "A sticky wicket then?"

He nodded. "Very much so."

"And I take it Justin wants to be a part of your family? At least get to know you and your sister better?"

"He does."

"Well, you can hardly fault his good taste, can you?"

she teased. "I mean, who wouldn't want you for a big brother? Come on. Former ranger, security expert, man with the plan," she said. "And I don't know your sister, but it sounds to me like you helped raise her. If that's the case, then she's got to be pretty remarkable, as well."

"She is," he said, his gaze twinkling with admiration.

Jess hesitated. "Can I make a suggestion?"

He lifted a sardonic brow. "Would it matter if I said no?"

"Ordinarily, no," she admitted because it was the truth. "But in this case, yes, it would." She grinned and leaned forward, as though sharing a little secret. "I'll admit that I've pressed you for answers, but we both know that if you really didn't want me to have them, then I wouldn't." She snorted indelicately and rolled her eyes. "You don't just play your cards close to your vest, you hide them beneath the table, and I am more than a little confident that even a firing squad at the ready couldn't make you give up your hand unless you chose to do so."

A bark of uncomfortable laughter erupted from his throat. "You think so, do you?"

"I don't think," she corrected. "I *know*." And he hated it, Jess thought, but she decided against pointing that out, as well. She liked unnerving him, but scaring the hell out of him was another matter altogether.

"You were going to make a suggestion?" he prompted, clearly uncomfortable with the direction their conversation had taken.

"Yes, I was," she said. "I understand your position and the fact that you don't want to needlessly hurt your mother or sister, but…they're adults, Griff, and Justin isn't." She bit her lip and softened her gaze. "He's a kid who's been through hell and you're his hero. And I just want to point out one more thing and then I swear, I'll shut up about it, but ask yourself this. If your father has been such a wonderful dad to him—when historically he's proven that he's not—then why is Justin trying so desperately to have a relationship with you? Is it because you gave him a kidney? Or could it be something else?"

He stilled, his gaze turning inward, then he looked at her and shook his head. "I…I don't know," he said. "Those are very good questions."

"I don't think that you have to make a choice between Justin and your mother and sister," she continued. "I think you should ask yourself if *you* want a relationship with your brother. And if that answer is yes, then let the chips fall where they may. Your family loves you. I can't imagine that they wouldn't want you to be happy."

She imagined it had been so long since he'd considered his own happiness, that putting others first had simply become second nature, that he no longer even considered his own wants and needs. Which was honorable, she'd admit, but hardly fair.

He glanced over at her, a wan smile on his distractingly sexy lips. "I'm sure you're right. Thanks," he added, almost as an afterthought, as though he wasn't accustomed to sharing his gratitude.

Jess grinned at him, then stood and straddled him, wrapping her arms around his neck and resting her forehead against his. "Anytime," she said, meaning it. She'd gladly be his confidante, particularly when she grimly suspected that he didn't have one.

She brushed her lips over his, reveling in the feel of his hands as they settled on her hips, and felt him instantly harden beneath her. Need coiled through her belly, making her breath stutter out of her lungs. She'd showered earlier and hadn't bothered to dress for bed, but had simply donned the hotel robe.

Best Decision Ever, she decided as his warm palms slid over her bare rump. Oh, how she loved his hands. They were large and long fingered, the backs of his knuckles sprinkled with fine auburn hair. Her feminine muscles tightened, slickening her folds, and she deepened the kiss, sucking his tongue into her mouth, deliberately mimicking a more intimate act. He groaned against her tongue, pushed his hands farther beneath her robe and then slid his fingers around until his thumbs brushed the undersides of her breasts. Gooseflesh skittered across her rapidly heating skin, pebbling her nipples. She dragged her lips from his, strung kisses along his jaw, the arch of his cheek, then nipped at his earlobe. He pushed up against her in response, the thin fabric of his boxers the only barrier between them.

And all of a sudden it was too much. Too damn much. She didn't want anything between them. Nothing separating them. She wanted to feel the full, hot, long length of him deep inside her, every ridge and vein, every gloriously proportioned inch.

She pushed her robe aside, baring herself to him, and it drooped around her shoulders, the sash gaping at the waist. His hot gaze feasted on her heavy breasts, then he cupped one and bent his beautiful head and sucked deeply, working his tongue against the sensitive point of her nipple.

Jess gasped, her lids fluttering shut from the pleasure, then she rocked her hips against him, riding the hard ridge of his arousal. It bumped against her sweet spot, sending another insistent wave of longing through her. "I've got a clean bill of health and I've got birth control covered," she said, her voice low and foggy. "You?"

"I'm clean," he said.

Oh, thank God, Jess thought, feeling as if she were about to fly into a million pieces. Her skin was too tight for her body, her clit throbbed with every frantic beat of her heart and need hammered through her, raw and desperate.

He reached between them, nudged the boxers down, freeing himself. The first touch of the thick crown of his penis against her weeping folds pulled the breath from her lungs and she didn't get it back until she'd lifted her hips and then impaled herself on him. Their gazes held and locked and for one limitless second the world receded, fell away, leaving only the two of them and this moment—this exquisite joining—and nothing else mattered.

Shaken to her core, Jess ignored the sudden strains of the wedding march as it cued up in her head and bent forward, finding his lips once more.

His kiss was different, still desperate, yes, but there was another quality there as well, one that made her eyes moisten with emotion and her heart sing.

Reverence.

He felt it, too, Jess thought, tightening around him, lifting her hips, then lowering again, the age-old rhythm taking hold as she frantically undulated her hips. Longing tangled through her, pooled and pounded against her womb, and every lurch of him deep inside her, every magnificent thrust of his hips pushed her closer and closer to the edge.

She could feel the tension mounting within him, felt it crackle around her like static, lifting the hairs off her arms, the back of her neck. His clever mouth worshipped her breasts, suckling, licking, laving, and his hands curled around her bottom, urging her on.

"Jesus, Jess— Please— I can't— I'm not going to— Come for me, baby," he begged her. "Let it go."

She whimpered. She was close, so close. Still… "You first."

"Jess," he said warningly. "Please. I'm dying. You're killing me."

She rode him harder, tightened around him, then reached around and slid a finger over the tight sack of his balls. "You *first.*"

His eyes widened. He sucked in a harsh breath, then he bucked violently beneath her. She felt him spasm inside her, a thick hot rush, bathing the back of her womb, and she came hard.

The orgasm took her unaware, ripping through her so viciously that her vision blackened around the edges, her heart skipped a few beats and every muscle in her body convulsed so thoroughly she developed cramps in her little toes. A low keening cry issued from her throat and she clung to him, held tightly, afraid that she might fly away or fall apart if she didn't.

Breathing raggedly, her belly still quaking, Jess finally drew back to look at him. His expression was a mix of awe and wonder, latent desire and satisfaction, and something else, something she struggled to define. But if she had to label it…*happy* was as good a word as any.

11

HAVING REVIEWED EVERY file he'd been given more than a dozen times as well as gone over routine updates on new check-ins and the guest list for the official event—he'd caught flak when he'd insisted that no other invitations were issued—Griff thought he was as prepared as he could possibly be.

Nothing out of the ordinary had happened at all last night—unless one counted the hours of mindless frantic sex, which he did, of course, but not as it pertained to his mission. His dick shifted as remembered heat curled into his loins.

As a rule, Griff didn't go bareback. Too much risk, either from an unwanted infection or pregnancy, neither of which made it onto his list of must-haves. But when Jess had crawled into his lap and settled her sweet sex against him and her robe had opened just enough to see the valley of her breasts and the V of sable curls hovering right over his dick...

He couldn't have made it to the bedroom for a condom if his life had depended on it. (He'd been saving the one with the elephant's trunk.) But...he'd just wanted her, needed her, more than he'd ever needed or wanted another woman before. Something about her just...drew him in, disabled the usual safeguards he'd always had in place, made him want to share his secrets and confess his fears, made him want to forget his plans—his schedule—and live in the moment with her.

That's what last night had been about—living.

Because if anyone knew how to live, it was Jess Rossi. Incredibly, the same hands that could craft some of the loveliest jewelry he'd ever seen could take an engine apart and rebuild it. She liked to drive fast, so she raced, despite the resistance of some of the other drivers. And, just when he'd thought nothing else about her could surprise him, he'd learned that she lived in a tree house. *A tree house, for God's sake!* When he'd asked her why, she'd merely shrugged and said why not.

Why not, indeed?

While most people conformed to convention, Jess fearlessly thumbed her nose at it and did as she pleased. Not in any way that would hurt other people, but in a way that made sure that she stayed true to herself.

She was remarkable, Griff thought, genuinely unique. And she had a singularly unique way of getting inside his head—terrifying, he'd admit—but also strangely...comforting. She didn't attempt to see through him, but instead really *looked*. It was a minute distinction, but one that was significant all the same.

A knock suddenly sounded on the door. No doubt that would be Andre, he thought. He'd annoyed the stylist to no end last night when he'd called him and insisted that Jess's hair and makeup be completed in their suite, but Griff refused to take any unnecessary risks. And the fact remained that they were safer in the room than anywhere else.

The biggest risk would come when they went downstairs to dress for the runway.

If it had been possible to do that in the room, too, he'd have insisted on that as well, but they were too far from the venue and the less time Jess spent in the bra the better. Since the Owl hadn't made his move last night, then logic demanded that he'd attempt to make the hit today.

Griff was ready.

He'd been over every inch of this floor, this hotel, all the schematics. He'd gone through every background history with anyone associated with this show, right down to the lowliest coffee gopher. He'd done everything he could possibly do to keep both Jess and the piece safe.

Confident of that, at the very least, he made sure the case was securely locked on his wrist and then pulled his gun from the back of his waistband.

"Is that really necessary?" Jess demanded from the bedroom doorway, her eyes wide.

"No chances," he told her, then carefully opened the door.

"Hello, Griff," Payne said, Flanagan and McCann on either side of him.

Griff blinked, stunned. "Hello," he said haltingly, unsure of what to make of their sudden appearance.

The three strolled in, nodded at Jess, who'd been freshly exfoliated this morning and was once again in the robe that he loved.

"After some discussion, we decided that this wasn't a one-man operation," Payne told him.

"Please don't think that we're questioning your capabilities, but in light of the threat and the fact that you're both part of the show now, we thought you could use additional backup."

Flanagan's gaze drifted around the room. "And Payne is secretly hoping that his old pal won't have the balls to steal something under his protection if he's actually visible."

Payne nodded. "There is that," he said. "I'm not certain that it'll make a difference, but on the off chance that it could…" He shrugged.

McCann settled into a chair, then leaned forward and inspected a map of the hotel. "Better numbers, better odds," he remarked. "Whereas he might be able to pick off one of us, it's unlikely that he could take down all three."

He was right, Griff decided, ignoring the twinge to his pride. They were right. He'd be a fool not to welcome additional help. He cleared his throat. "Thank you for coming," he said to the room at large. "I appreciate it."

A second knock sounded and Griff repeated his earlier process, then ushered Andre and a couple of pre-screened hotel staffers, their arms loaded down with various cases, into the suite.

"It's you," Andre remarked, staring intently at Griff.

"From the elevator. I never forget a face, even when it's attached to someone else's," he added with a droll little smile, much to Griff's discomfort.

From the corner of his eye he watched Flanagan grin, McCann lift a brow and Payne's lips twitch. He decided he'd have to figure out what to make of that later.

"And if you're you, then I can only assume that—" His gaze landed on Jess and he slapped his hands together delightedly, making his jewelry rattle. "Oh, yes!" he exclaimed. "Yes, yes, yes! That skin! That hair! No extensions for you, my lovely," he gushed in rapturous tones. "Where am I setting up?" he asked Griff without looking at him, his gaze still clinging to Jess.

"The master bath, through there," Griff told him.

"Excellent." He whirled around and clapped twice. "Chop, chop," he said. "You heard the man. Through there."

And then with a smile that was as uncertain as excited, Jess glanced at him, shrugged helplessly and followed Andre.

"I'm assuming he's been thoroughly checked out," Payne commented.

Griff pulled the appropriate file and handed it to him. "This is what I got from Charlie, along with what I managed to find on my own. Andre Wiltmon, thirty-three, born and raised in Philadelphia."

Payne blinked, surprised. "He's a Harvard graduate. Journalism."

"Yes, I saw that. According to his website, he started on one side of fashion, but found his calling on the other. He's got quite a client list." He reeled off a few Hollywood A-listers. "Oh, and Prince," he added.

McCann grinned. "That one actually makes sense."

Seemingly satisfied, Payne nodded and gestured to the table. "All right, let's go through all this one more time, then we'll put together an action plan."

Griff grinned. Ah, he thought. A plan. Music to his ears.

PRACTICALLY QUIVERING WITH joy, Andre leaned back and beamed at her. "You're stunning, darling. Absolutely freaking *stunning.*"

Jess didn't know about that, particularly as Andre had put her back to the mirror and refused to let her turn around. He'd spent the past hour and a half working on her hair and makeup, had wielded the blow-dryer, flat iron and makeup brushes as weapons against mediocrity—his words, not hers—and had elevated her natural-born beauty into something *more.* Jess's lips quirked with droll humor.

Andre was all about more.

One more curl, one more pluck of the tweezers, one more hit of bronzer. More, more, more.

"So what's the story with you and Captain Badass out there?" he asked, smoothing out an errant hair that had caught his critical eye. "Are y'all just making the beast with two backs, or is it more?"

Jess felt her eyes widen and she made a little strangling sound. "I'm sorry, what?"

"Don't play coy with me, missy," he said, wagging a pair of eyelash curlers at her. "I'm not blind. I saw the pair of you in the elevator, remember, when you were trying to inspect his tonsils with your tongue. But if that wasn't a big enough clue, then the condom wrappers in the bedside trash and the empty bottle of massage oil on the nightstand definitely told the whole story. Besides, sex has a certain smell," he continued almost philosophically. "It hit me like a two-by-four the minute I walked into the suite. And through the bedroom. And in here as well, if I'm being completely honest." He smiled down at her, lifting an impressed brow. "You've been a busy girl. I'm surprised you've got the strength to do the show."

Oh, good Lord, Jess thought. She'd been mildly concerned about Griff's bosses showing up unannounced, but had hoped that they'd be so distracted by their need to protect the bra that they wouldn't notice that there wasn't a blanket on the living room sofa or that two people had obviously slept in the bed the previous night.

But if Andre had noticed, then she was relatively certain that they had, as well. She hoped she didn't get Griff into trouble, she fretted. She wasn't sure what sort of fraternization rules they had, but she'd be willing to assume all the blame to keep him from any sort of recriminations.

"Well?" he prodded. "Is he a keeper or are you going to throw him back?"

He was definitely a keeper, but circumstances being what they were, she didn't see how they'd be able to continue seeing each other beyond this weekend. The realist in her wouldn't let her think otherwise. And because of that, she planned on taking advantage of every minute she spent with him. She wanted to make love to him over and over again, but more important, she wanted to give him a little bit of happiness, to put that expression she'd noticed on his face last night more often—if not permanently, then at least enough to make it familiar to him.

If he took anything away from her this weekend—aside from her heart—then she wanted it to be a lesson in joy, in chasing after his own, specifically.

"Fine." Andre huffed playfully. "Don't tell me then. But I saw the way he looked at you and I will say this," he offered. "I think that hook is good and set. You could easily reel him in if you were so inclined."

"How's your little dog?" Jess asked, deliberately changing the subject.

He blinked, smiled. "She's fine, thanks for asking. Now, are you ready to look in the mirror?"

Her stomach gave a little jump. "I don't know, am I?"

In answer, Andre whirled her chair around and crouched over her shoulder. "Ta da!"

Jess watched her eyes and mouth round simultaneously and she sucked in a strangled breath. "Holy crap on a cracker," she breathed.

"I *know*," he said with a pleased nod. "You're breathtaking. You're going to knock the shine right off that bra, sweetheart."

She didn't know about that, but she definitely looked better than she ever had in her life. Her hair was full, with big smooth curls, and it hung neatly over her shoulders and puddled just shy of the tops of her breasts. Her makeup was flawless. Dramatic, but still subtle—a neat trick, she had to admit—and she had a definite glow about her, as though she were lit from within.

"Wow," she said shakily, meeting his heavily lined gaze in the mirror. "Thank you."

He managed a humble nod. "You're welcome." He squeezed her shoulders. "Now, pull it together, darling. It's showtime."

Oh, dear Lord. She'd actually managed to forget why they'd gone to all this trouble. The reminder made her stomach lurch.

Having exchanged the short robe for a longer one to make the journey from here to the ballroom—which curiously enough made her more squeamish than walking a runway in nothing but a bra and a pair of boy-short panties—she stood on shaky legs and followed Andre back into the living room.

Conversation stopped and four sets of eyes swung in her direction, but Griff's naturally were the pair she sought out.

He'd stopped midsentence, his jaw hanging open, and his blue-green gaze flared with appreciation and heat. "Jesus, Jess," he breathed, evidently forgetting himself.

"You look beautiful, Ms. Rossi," Payne told her, pushing to his feet, and the rest of them followed suit.

"Gorgeous," Flanagan chimed in.

"Lovely," McCann added.

Jess swallowed, felt a blush climb her neck. "Thank you."

Andre bussed the lightest kiss against her cheek. "I

need to go down and check on the other girls," he said. "I'll see you downstairs." He looked at Griff. "Would you mind having my gear delivered backstage, please? You banished my helpers," he drawled. "Otherwise they could have done it."

Griff nodded. "I'll see to it."

With another encouraging look in her direction, Andre took his leave. Griff made the call to see to the stylist's things, then took a bracing breath and arched a brow. "Ready?"

"I'm as ready as I'm ever going to be."

Griff took the spot next to her, then Flanagan led, Payne flanked Griff and McCann brought up the rear. They took the service elevator down to the ballroom floor, where a pair of Clandestine associates with clipboards and stressed attitudes met them and led them to the staging area. Half-naked models were everywhere—a visual reminder that she didn't look anything like them at all, quickly undermining her confidence. Music blared to a near-deafening level and lights swung in every direction, giving a nightclub vibe. Griff followed her into the flimsy dressing room—she'd insisted that he be the only one with her when she changed—and removed the cuff from his wrist, then the bra from the case.

Heart hammering in her throat, hands shaking, she shrugged carefully into it and he just as carefully connected the hooks. His fingers were warm, slightly unsteady, and when she met his eyes in the mirror, his gaze was blistering hot with need, tempered with affection. "Do you have any idea how much I want to kiss you?" he asked softly. "Any idea at all?"

Probably as much as she wanted him to, Jess thought, bolstered by his obvious appreciation. "You can't," she said regretfully. "Andre would flip a bitch if you messed up my lipstick."

He snorted. "Andre can go to hell."

"Andre doesn't want to go to hell," the man himself announced, stepping into the little room. "Andre wants to go to the bar and get hammered because Andre is sick of dealing with temperamental supermodels with limited vocabularies, daddy issues and an exaggerated sense of self-importance," he said. "But that, too, will have to wait." He shooed Griff. "Go," he told him. "Sophia is going to help you get ready."

Griff frowned. "I don't need any help. I can dress myself, thanks."

He laughed. "Not for a runway you can't. Your other friends are right outside the curtain," he said. "Now, scoot."

Jess had to admit that watching Griff get bossed around by a man who'd likely had more manicures than she had was a sight to behold, and more than a little funny.

His blue-green gaze caught and held hers. "I'll see you in a minute," he said.

She nodded.

The second Griff stepped out, Payne stepped in, making Andre roll his eyes. He huffed dramatically. "Oh, for pity's sake," he groused. "What do you think I'm going to do? Conk her on the head, whisk her away to some tropical location and sacrifice her to the volcano gods?"

Payne didn't reply, to which Andre leaned forward and said, "He's a chatty one, isn't he? Personality *galore*."

Jess met Payne's gaze in the mirror and was surprised when he winked at her.

Andre fussed around her, tweaking a hair here and there, then swiped a bit of powder over her cheeks. "There," he said. "You're perfect." He quickly produced his phone, loaded the camera and slung an arm over her shoulder. He leaned in close and grinned. "Smile," he said, aiming the phone an arm's length away, then snapped a picture. "I always like having a selfie of my work," he said.

Jess merely nodded.

Andre's eyes suddenly rounded. "That's your cue," he said, hurrying her out of the room.

She dimly noted Payne, Flanagan and McCann, then caught sight of Griff and her heart jumped into an erratic beat. Dressed in a classic tuxedo, his curls smoothed into a sleek forties-era style, he looked impossibly handsome and mouthwateringly sexy. His blue-green eyes were rife with uncertainty—a phenomenon, she was sure—and when he smiled, the ground shifted a little beneath her feet.

"You clean up nice," she said, giving him a lengthy lingering once-over.

He leaned forward. "Stop looking at me like that," he warned under his breath. "Or I'm going to ruin the line of these slacks."

She grinned.

Headset in place, Clarice hurried over, then steered them toward the back of the runway. "Okay," she said. "You know what you're doing, right? Shoulders back, head up and walk like you're on a mission." She turned to Griff. "You're the slathering hound on her heels," she told him. "You're the dog after her bone. While you're watching her walk away, you're admiring everything about her. You want her so desperately you can taste it. Can you do it?"

His humorous gaze tangled with hers. "Oh, I think I can handle it."

"Excellent." She cast a glance toward the curtain, nodded when she received the signal. "All right. You're up. Go."

Because the bra was the finale piece of the show-case, Jess was supposed to work all three runways, giving everyone in the room an ample view of the piece. This was it, she told herself, the moment her father had worked so very hard for. A flash of images fired through her brain, all of them of him—his head bent over the bra, tools in hand, stretching his aching back, his happy expression when he'd completed a section he was especially proud of.

This was for her dad, she thought determinedly. And with Griff at her side, she could do anything. Even walk half-naked out into a room full of strangers. She lifted her head, drew her shoulders back and strode forward. Jess worked that runway as if she owned it. She smiled and preened, she blew kisses at Griff, purposely sent him a few slaying sidelong glances, and by the time she took her final bow, the entire room was on its feet—some of them on their chairs—and the applause was so loud it drowned out the music.

Griff leaned over. "I think you might have missed your calling," he whispered.

"You, too, Spot."

"Spot?"

She sent him a wicked look. "You're my dog, aren't you?"

His eyes flashed. "Damn straight. And I'm looking forward to humping the hell out of you later."

Jess grinned, a thrill whipping through her. "Not as much as I'm looking forward to clipping a leash to your neck."

12

HIS EARS STILL ringing from Jess's "leash" comment and the applause, Griff scanned the audience, ever mindful of the threat, and snugged a finger against her back. He'd noticed Flanagan and McCann in the audience and fully expected Payne to be waiting for them when they came off the runway. "Come on," he said. "We need to move."

Her nod was imperceptible, but he caught it and, smiling at the room at large, she turned and began retracing her steps. They both heaved a big sigh of relief when they took the last step—Griff because that was one hurdle crossed, Jess presumably because she'd gotten her modeling debut over with.

The whole backstage area erupted into wild applause the instant they saw Jess. Andre clapped wildly, Clarice beamed at her and both Mr. Pershing and Mr. Nolan wore admiring grins.

"You were magnificent," Mr. Pershing told her. "Well done, my dear. Well done."

"You must come to the after party," Mr. Nolan insisted. "Even if it's only for a few minutes."

Her hesitant gaze swung to Griff's and she arched a brow.

He nodded, unable to deny her the well-deserved moment of glory. "Just for a few minutes," he said. "I'll go up and get everything ready to go."

Though the original plan had involved the bra going on the model for the evening cocktail party, Griff had nixed that element and had decided that the sooner the repairs were made to the piece and it was delivered back into the hands of the Montwheeler representative, the better.

Because Mr. Rossi wasn't going to leave his store, the repairs had to be made on-site. But the actual hand-off would be done in Atlanta, at the Ranger Security offices. He wasn't exactly certain whether Payne, Flanagan and McCann were going to follow them, but he assumed they would, if for no other reason than to see this case through to the end.

It took Griff several minutes to steer Jess back to her dressing room to change, but when the bra was once again stored safely in its case and handcuffed to Griff's wrist, she turned and pressed a long, thorough kiss on his lips.

"Thank you," she murmured when at last she drew back.

Griff grinned and shook his head. "Tell me what I did and I'll do it again."

"I couldn't have done that without you," she said.

"When you look at me, you make me feel beautiful. You make me believe it."

"First of all, yes, you most definitely could have done it without me because you're the bravest woman I know. And that's saying something," he added, "because I know a lot of brave people." He slid a finger down her cheek. "Second, Jess, you *are* beautiful." He shook his head, genuinely mystified. "I don't know why you think you aren't."

"It's not that I think I'm not," she said. "But knowing it and feeling it are two completely different things. *You* make me feel it. Just you."

"Griff?" Payne's voice called through the curtain before he could respond.

"Coming," he said.

"We'll finish this discussion later," he told her. "Remember, only stay a few minutes. We need to get on the road." He paused. "Would you like one of the guys to come with you? I can—"

She shook her head. "It's you he's going to be after," she said. "Not me. Take them with you. I'll be fine."

He knew that she was right, yet he hesitated.

"Griff, go," she encouraged, giving him a little push. "I'm not what he wants."

No, but she was what *he* wanted, he thought, momentarily paralyzed as the notion flitted easily through his head. His mouth parched and panic punched him hard in the chest.

"Griff?" she asked, her smooth brow clouding with concern. "Are you all right? You look funny."

He shook himself. "I'm fine. I'll, uh...I'll see you upstairs."

Determined to think about anything but the little earth-shattering realization he'd just come to, Griff hurried out and found Payne, McCann and Flanagan waiting for him.

"You should have taken the tux off before clipping that to your wrist," McCann said. "Good job, by the way. You play the role of 'slathering hound' quite well," he added, a faint smile on his lips.

Irritated, Griff glanced at the top of McCann's head and stared until the other man frowned. "What?" he asked.

"It must be invisible," Griff remarked as they boarded the service elevator.

McCann scowled. "What's invisible?"

"Your dick hat," he said. "I know it's there because you're running your mouth, but I can't see it."

Payne grinned and Flanagan chuckled. "Dick hat," Flanagan repeated, rocking back on his heels. "I'm *so* stealing that."

"Enough, gentlemen," Payne told them. "If Keller's still going to make a move, then it's going to be in the next few minutes."

Griff glanced at him. "What makes you so sure?"

He shot him a mild look. "Because that's how I'd do it."

"Me, too," McCann said after a small pause. "It's made its debut, the buzz has started. What better way to increase the value?"

"He's not interested in increasing the value," Payne said. "He's giving it back, remember?"

"He *says* he'll give it back," Flanagan pointed out. He winced skeptically. "But I have to tell you, I have a hard time putting my trust into the word of a thief."

"Just because he's a thief, that doesn't mean he's a liar," Payne told him. "If he says he'll give it back, then he'll give it back."

"You honestly believe that?" McCann asked him.

Payne nodded once. "I do."

"How about we just don't let him take it to start with?" Griff interjected. "I like that plan."

Flanagan slipped him a high five. "I do, too."

They finished the ride up to the sixteenth floor in silence, then exited, their guns drawn, careful to keep a close watch for anything out of the ordinary. Griff had slipped Payne the room key card earlier and it was he who inserted it into the lock. The suite was quiet when they entered, almost eerily so, but a thorough search revealed that they were alone and all was as it should be.

Griff released a tense breath. "I'm going to change," he told them. "Somebody give me an arm."

Payne offered his. Once the case was securely locked onto Payne's wrist, Griff excused himself to go into the bedroom and quickly swapped the tux for a pair of jeans and a sweater. He'd just started packing up when suddenly the television came on in the bathroom.

He frowned, pulled his Glock from the back of his pants and peered into the room.

Nothing.

"Welcome to Owl TV," a voice said from the screen. "Trust me. You'll give a hoot."

Owl TV? A prickling of unease slid up his spine and camped at the base of his neck. Anticipation spiked, quickening his pulse. "Payne," Griff called quietly.

"Yes, yes, do call Payne," the voice continued. "I'm looking forward to seeing him. He's an old friend, you know."

What the hell? How was the damn television *talking* to him? Griff edged farther into the room to better see the television set. An image of a great horned owl perched on a thick tree branch filled the screen.

"Come on in," the owl said, its beak moving as though it was actually speaking. "Don't be shy. It's important that all of you hear this."

Payne, Flanagan and McCann all warily filed in and he watched as each of their faces registered the same grim shock he was feeling himself.

"Payne," the bird said warmly. "It's been a long time."

Payne's face was an unreadable mask, his gaze cool. "Where are you, Keller?"

"That's classified information, soldier," he said. "But don't worry, we'll get a chance to catch up soon. For the moment, you simply need to listen. I'm going to take that lovely bra off your wrist, keep it for forty-eight hours, then I'll return it personally to you at a location I'll share with you at a later time. You'll need to come alone, of course. You were never a snitch and I doubt that you are now, but better safe than sorry, I always say."

Griff had heard enough. "Listen, I don't know who the hell you think you are, but—"

The owl tsked and shook his head. "It's rude to interrupt, Mr. Wicklow." The great head turned back toward Payne. "Now, as I was saying, as a show of good faith, I'm leaving something in exchange for what I'm taking, of equal value, of course. And I have arranged an online auction for my piece, which is far from a Rossi, I'll admit, but quite nice all the same. The auction will automatically commence in two hours. Payne, the auction company will only release the funds to you and you're to give the money to the charity or charities of your choice. I, personally, prefer to make donations to agencies that help battered and abused children, but that's just me." He paused. "I'm looking forward to catching up."

The screen went black, the bathroom door suddenly swung closed and the room instantly filled with a smoky sweet gas.

"Son of a bitch," Flanagan muttered, a sentiment that was echoed in one form or another by the rest of them.

They all bolted into action, stumbled toward the door, but none of them even so much as reached the handle. One minute Griff was covering his mouth with his sleeve, the next...the world went black.

When he awoke, it was to the frantic shaking of Jess's arms on his shoulders, the sight of her pale, tear-stained terrified face and a violent headache.

"Griff?" A tear splashed on his cheek. "Griff? Oh, please, Griff," she sobbed, sliding a hand over his face. "Please don't be— I couldn't bear it—" He felt her lips against his skin, her wet lashes brush against him, and he struggled to open his eyes, to let her know that he was okay. He groaned, blinked, and he felt her stiffen.

"Griff?"

"Shh," he told her, his voice weak. "Don't cry."

Her hands moved lovingly over his face. "Oh, Griff. Oh, thank God," she said, her voice broken and thick with still-unshed tears. "You're all right. I thought you were—" She hugged him tightly and he could feel her shaking with fear, her slender shoulders trembling. "But you're not— You're all r-right."

It took a few seconds for his fuzzy brain to catch up, but when it did, his gaze darted around the bathroom, saw Payne, Flanagan and McCann all on the floor as well, but beginning to stir.

"Knockout gas," McCann said a few minutes later, bathing his face with a wet cloth Jess had gotten for him. "That's some wicked shit."

After confirming that the bra was, in fact, gone and had been replaced with another, this one a snowy owl design, which was primarily set with diamonds, pearls and varying shades of topaz, they'd all moved to the living room. There was something rather pathetic about lingering in the bathroom, McCann had pointed out, and the air was cleaner.

Looking distinctly green around the gills again— he'd already emptied his stomach twice—Flanagan glared at Payne. "Fair warning. Old friend or not, I'm going to track that bastard down to the ends of the earth if necessary and beat the bloody hell out of him."

Griff snorted. "I'll join you."

Not because he'd bested all four of them or out of any sense of impugned honor, but for Jess, who'd been terrified that she'd walked in on a quadruple homicide and was at the very moment wiping a tear from her cheek, saddened over the loss of her father's work.

He pulled her closer and pressed a kiss against her head, not caring who saw him. "He's returning it to Payne, Jess. In two days."

"I know," she said. "I just dread telling my father. He worked so hard on it. Remember what he said about the piece securing the Rossi legacy." She offered him a watery smile. "I don't think this is what he had in mind."

"Maybe not," Payne told her. "But if his angle was exposure for your company, then having the piece stolen by the infamous Owl will certainly get him that. More than if it had never been lifted to start with." He grimaced. "The press is going to have a field day and the only company involved that is going to come out of this looking like incompetent fools is Ranger Security. Because we let him take it. We failed."

Every startled gaze in the room swung to Payne.

"We were *gassed,* Payne," McCann said tightly. "I'm not willing to call that a failure. I call that foul play."

"Call it whatever you want, but we lost the cargo. We are no longer in possession of the item we were hired to protect."

"No, but we're in possession of something of equal value and we're insured," Jamie added. "Furthermore, there's the confidentiality agreement. No one knows Ranger Security was tapped to provide protection. Neither Clandestine nor Montwheeler is going to divulge that information. They'd be in breach of contract and we'd sue the hell out of them."

"You don't think it's going to get leaked?"

McCann lifted his chin. "I think that if it does, we have the resources to track down the source—who could only be associated with one company or the other—and file suit. I think that when we meet with both parties, we need to make that little tidbit painfully clear."

Payne nodded. "I agree." He glanced at Jess and lifted a brow. "Would you mind telling us exactly what you saw as you came back upstairs, in the elevator, the hall, and when you came into the suite?"

"Of course," she said. "I, uh…I went to the service elevator, but after several minutes, when the call button didn't respond, I walked to the lobby and got on the Barry White elevator. I—"

"The Barry White elevator?" Flanagan asked incredulously.

Jess blushed and shot Griff a look. "It's the elevator that always comes for us," she said. "The very last one on the right and the music is…"

"Baby-making music," Griff finished for her. "George Michael, Marvin Gaye and Barry White."

"And that's the only elevator that ever responded to your call? There was never any instrumental Muzak playing?" McCann asked in amazement. He grimaced significantly and shook his head. "He's been screwing with you from the beginning, hasn't he?"

Griff stilled, then swore. Of course he had. Anyone with the audiovisual skills required to manipulate the cable and stream a damn *talking owl* into the room could have easily influenced the elevators and music.

"Let's get back to Ms. Rossi," Payne said, urging her to continue.

"Anyway, I rode up the elevator. I was alone and it didn't stop for anyone else, then I walked down to our room."

"Did you see anyone in the hall?"

She bit her lip, considered the question, then shook her head. "No, not a soul. Not even any of the house-keeping staff."

"Okay, go on."

"When I got to the room, I realized that I didn't have a key, so I lifted my hand to knock. That's when I noticed it lying on the floor, just beneath the edge of the door."

"The key card?"

"Yes."

"So he wanted her to be able to get in and find us quickly," Flanagan remarked.

"How thoughtful of him," McCann drawled.

"And then what?" Payne asked.

"Well...the first thing I noticed when I came in was that weird smell," she said. "It was sweet."

"The gas," Griff told her.

"I thought that it was odd that you weren't in here," she said, gesturing to the living room area. "And then I heard someone call my name and say, 'Back here.'"

Payne leaned forward, his gaze sharpening. "You heard someone call your name? Where did it sound like it was coming from?"

"The bathroom," she said. "I thought it was Griff, but…"

All of them shared a look as a key piece fell into place.

"He was still here," Griff said.

Flanagan whistled low. "He waited for Jess to get back, then he sneaked out as soon as she found us in the bathroom, when she was distracted."

"Ballsy bastard," McCann said. "What if she'd run out screaming?"

"He did his homework," Griff said, reluctantly impressed. "He knew she wouldn't run. She's not afraid of anything."

She smiled at him and leaned over. "You keep forgetting the clowns," she said. "But thank you, anyway."

"When you found us," Payne prompted. "Was the bathroom door opened or closed?"

"Open," she said. "The vent was on. You were all on the floor," she said. "Near the door. And the new case was on your wrist and the owl feather was on top of your chest."

"If you think of anything else, no matter how insignificant you think it might be, please tell us."

Jess nodded. "I will."

Payne thanked her, then pushed to his feet and started looking around. "All right," he said. "Let's get to work, gentlemen. Where the hell did he hide? How the hell did he do it?"

The four of them fanned out, started sweeping the suite once again. Griff found a tiny camera mounted to the top of the television screen, which accounted for how he'd known who was in the bathroom. He'd been watching. McCann located the source of the gas—the canisters had been placed in the floor vents, which had been blocked off. Keller had remote detonated them. And Flanagan and Payne found his hiding place—the box springs beneath the bed. He'd torn away the thin fabric from the bottom and climbed up between the slats.

"No way," McCann said, crouching low to look beneath the bed.

"Way," Jamie told him. "I'm the biggest one here and I can do it."

He did.

Jess bit her lip and darted a look at Griff. "You don't think he's been hiding under there the whole time, do you?"

Griff shook his head. "I very seriously doubt it."

"I do, too," Payne told her. "He'd only need a few minutes in here to do what he needed to do," he said. "He wouldn't have hidden in here long. Too risky."

"Do you think the surveillance tapes are going to be of any use at all?" McCann asked.

"I doubt it, but we should look at them." He glanced at Griff. "In the interim, I think that you and Ms. Rossi should head back to Shadow's Gap and let the three of us wrap things up here. Once you've got her settled and brought her father up to speed, you can return to Atlanta." He turned to Jess. "Ms. Rossi, the instant we have the piece back, you can rest assured that we will return it to your father for the repairs, then make sure that it's delivered to Montwheeler."

She nodded. "I have every confidence in that, Mr. Payne."

"It's Brian," he said, shooting her a smile.

She and Griff made quick work of packing up, said their goodbyes, then rather than wait on the valet to pull the SUV around, made their way to the parking garage. They'd barely settled into the seats when Jess turned to him.

"There's no way in hell you're taking me back to Shadow's Gap, not without that damn bra. I'm coming to Atlanta with you."

Griff grinned at her. "I never doubted it."

13

"ARE YOU SURE you don't want me to drive?" Jess asked, her gaze clinging to Griff's profile. "I don't mind at all and I know that awful gas had to have made you a little sick."

"I'm over it now," he assured her. "No worries."

"Are you sure you're all right?" Honestly, when she'd come around the corner and caught a glimpse of his prone frame on the bathroom floor, she'd come as close to fainting as she ever hoped to. Her heart had dropped to her feet, the blood had rushed out of her head, roaring past her ears, and her mouth had gone bone dry.

And he thought she was fearless.

She'd never known terror like that, had never been more afraid of anything in her life. The idea that he was gone—God help her, dead—had took hold and she hadn't been able to shake it off until he'd moaned and blinked those amazing eyes up at her.

He reached over and squeezed her hand. "Jess, I'm

fine, really. The only thing that was wounded was my pride and it'll recover. Eventually," he drawled.

"It was a damn sneaky thing to do," she said. "How were you supposed to counter that? You were prepared to meet him face-to-face, not have him hide beneath the bed and blast you all with an incapacitating agent."

He shot her a look, smiled. "Incapacitating agent?"

She cocked her head, darting him a pointed look. "I've watched enough crime dramas to know what knockout gas is, smart-ass."

"I'll just bet you have," he muttered, still grinning.

"So…what's the plan?"

He lifted a brow. "The plan? Other than driving until we don't feel like driving anymore, I don't have one."

No plan? Wow, they had made some progress, she thought, pleased. "You aren't going to do anything sneaky, like try to take me back to Shadow's Gap, are you?" she asked, suddenly suspicious.

He chuckled and shook his head. "No, of course not. You said you didn't want to go back, that you wanted to come with me to Atlanta."

"Will it be a problem for you?" she asked hesitantly. "You know, with Payne and the others?"

"Would it matter if it was?" he asked.

"Not to me," she said. "But they're your coworkers and I don't know what your company fraternization rules are."

"Well, considering that each one of them—and nearly every other agent who works for them—all met their spouses on the job, then I seriously doubt they'll have anything to say about you."

Jess felt her eyes widen. "Seriously?"

He nodded once. "Seriously."

She hummed under her breath. "Well, good. I would have gone to a hotel if it had been a problem, but I'd rather stay with you." She reached over and patted him on the head. "I've grown rather fond of my hound," she teased.

He rolled his eyes, snorted. "Rather fond, huh? Does that mean I'm going to get a treat later?"

Jess reached over and cupped him through his jeans, smiling when he jumped and his jaw tensed. "Who said anything about later?"

"Jess," he said warningly as she slid the button from its closure and lowered his zipper.

She bent over and peeked up at him from lowered lashes. "This thing has tinted windows, right? I don't want to inadvertently give some trucker a show."

"Government grade," he said, sucking in a breath as she freed him. He shifted, hit the back button on his power seat, sliding it farther from the steering wheel.

Jess pulled her hair out of the way, tucking it over one shoulder, then ran her tongue around the soft rim of his engorged head, before pulling the whole crown into her mouth.

He swore violently, tensing his legs.

"Do you want me to stop?" she teased, licking the length of him, the musky scent of man filling her nostrils.

"No."

Good, because she didn't want to. She loved the way he felt in her mouth, the soft, soft skin, the thick veins running along his long, hard shaft. She wrapped her lips around him again, flicked her tongue against the V of his head, hitting the sensitive spot just beneath the rim of the crown, and sucked hard, dragging him deeper and deeper into her mouth.

She could feel the tension tightening the muscles in his legs, the sound of his harsh breath gasping between his teeth. His balls hardened, drawing up against her palm and she worked his shaft with the other, chasing her strokes with mouth. She caught the first taste of him on her tongue and sighed with pleasure, then upped the tempo and sucked harder, took him deeper, opening her throat to accommodate his massive size.

"Jess, I can't— I'm going to—"

"Come for me, baby," she breathed, giving him the same order he'd given her last night.

As though those were the magic words, he did. She lapped it up, licked him clean, kept feeding at him until the very last bit was milked out of him, then pressed a lingering kiss on the crown of his cock and sat up.

"I thoroughly enjoyed that," she said.

Seemingly shocked, his expression was one of frozen delight. "You, uh…You didn't have to, you know," he said, gesturing awkwardly.

Jess felt her lips twitch. "I liked it better than the alternative," she said.

"Oh? What was that?"

"Getting it in my hair," she replied with a naughty grin. "My hair is looking especially good today."

"Everything about you looks especially good every

day," he said. "But I have to admit, you were magnificent on that runway. You *owned* it."

"You weren't too bad yourself," she said, pleasure blooming in her chest at the unexpected praise. She slid him a look. "We make a good team."

He smiled, then reached over and took her hand again, giving it a squeeze. "Yes, we do," he said. He glanced at her, his gaze lingering on her face. "Why don't you try to get some rest," he said. "We're in for a long drive."

"I'll be fine," she assured him.

Famous last words, she thought hours later. It was after dark when she awoke, the moon hanging low in the sky, and they were in a parking lot of a popular hotel chain.

"Hello, Sleeping Beauty," he teased, sliding a hand over her cheek.

Jess stretched, yawned. "I'm sorry," she said. "I didn't mean to play out on you."

"No problem," he assured her, his gaze dropping to her lips. "I'd rather you have plenty of rest for tonight."

She smiled. "Gonna need my strength, am I? That sounds promising, though I do hope you're planning to feed me first. I'm hungry."

"I've ordered something," he said, pulling around to the back of the building. He helped her with her bag, then located their room and opened the door. It was a substantial downgrade from the honeymoon suite, but it was clean and comfortable and they were together.

Win, win, win.

Their dinner arrived in short order, then they had

each other for dessert. Jess was pleasantly exhausted, her limbs still trembling from another one of those magnificent orgasms he always managed to pull from her body, when Griff decided to turn the television on...

And she saw the pair of them making their runway debut. She sat bolt upright and scrambled to the end of the bed. "We're on the news? Already?" she asked, her voice climbing. "Damn, that was quick."

"There's no such thing as bad publicity," Griff said. "I know you're worried about this being bad for business, but Payne was right. If anything, it'll be just the opposite. For Rossi jewelry, Clandestine and Montwheeler."

They watched the whole piece, thankful when the reporter glossed over how the bra was actually stolen, probably because they hadn't been given the details. Evidently Payne's confidentiality warning was effective.

She sighed and looked over at Griff. "No mention of Ranger Security. That's a good thing, right?"

"Definitely." He'd pulled out his laptop and turned it around to show her. "The bra the Owl substituted is already up to four hundred and fifty thousand dollars," he said. "And there's still another day left on the auction."

She'd inspected it before they'd left. "It's a damn fine piece of work," she said. "Not as good as anything me or my father could make, quite honestly, but still, very good. It's well designed, the cast is fine and each of the jewels is competently set. If he did it himself, then that's impressive. It takes years of practice to be able to execute something to that degree."

Griff lifted a bare shoulder. "He intimated that he did it himself, also admitting that it wasn't as well done as a Rossi."

"Well, he got one part of that right, at any rate. Do you think he's telling the truth?"

"Payne insists that being a thief doesn't make him a liar, and he trusts him," he said. Griff hesitated, seemingly unsure.

"But you don't?" she asked.

"I don't know him, but Brian Payne is nobody's fool. If Payne trusts him, then I have to believe that trust isn't misplaced." He turned to look at her, his eyes guarded, wary. "Speaking of misplaced trust, I'm sorry," he said.

Jess blinked, confused. He was sorry? "Sorry for what?"

"For losing the piece when I promised that I wouldn't." He shook his head. "You trusted me and I—"

Jess scrambled onto his lap and took his dear face into her hands. "And I still trust you," she said, pinning him with her gaze. "You are not to blame for what happened, you hear me? You did everything you possibly could to keep this from happening. I don't know what you could have done that might have resulted in a different outcome."

He smiled sadly, a weary grin on his mouth. "I don't either, but I still feel like a fool."

"I'm sure that Payne, Flanagan and McCann all feel like fools as well, but do you think they are?"

"What? No," he said, as though the idea was ludicrous.

She smiled, rested her forehead against his. "My point exactly."

Humor lit his gaze and the corner of his mouth hitched up, tugging into a half grin that was extremely endearing and equally sexy. He sighed, almost as though he'd come to some sort of inevitable conclusion. "You're good for my ego," he told her.

He was good for hers, as well. "Ditto," she said, melting with happiness.

It was nice to be here with him without the case, without the mission, without any purpose other than to get back to Atlanta. Without a plan, she thought, her grin widening.

Griff lifted his head and kissed her, his lips sliding mesmerizingly over hers. He tasted like barbecue and hot apple pie, like sin and seduction, like home and, God help her, happily ever after.

"Hey, Jess?"

"Hmm?"

"Would it be all right if I made hot sweet love to you all night long?" he asked, his voice low and husky.

She wrapped her arms around his neck, pressed herself more firmly against him and sighed softly into his mouth. "Oh, hell, yes."

CLAD IN ONE of Griff's long-sleeved flannel shirts, her knees drawn up to her chest, hair tumbling over her shoulders, Jess sat on the end of his couch, her gaze riveted to the television. The Owl's theft of the bra hadn't been the only thing that had the media in an uproar.

She was.

News agencies and daytime talk-show hosts played the clip of her runway appearance repeatedly, rejoicing that Clandestine had allowed her, a "normal" woman, to model their most exquisite, most anticipated piece of the year.

"Just look at her," one woman remarked. "She's got *confidence,* she's got *curves,* she's *gorgeous,* but it's more than that. She's somehow managed to embody, in just a few short steps, the power of being a woman, of celebrating femininity."

"Or it could be that super-hot guy chasing after her, Nina," her cohost joked.

The pair laughed and then they launched into their critique of Griff's performance, which was not getting as much attention as Jess's, but more than enough to warrant lots of phone calls from friends and family, most especially Justin, whom he was talking to right now.

"You're on every channel!" the boy said, his voice going high. "Seriously, dude. *Every* channel. Like the president."

Griff chuckled, unable to help himself in the face of Justin's awed delight.

"You didn't mention that your new job involved escorting supermodels," he gushed. "I thought you were in the security business."

"I am," he said. "But there are aspects of my job that I'm not at liberty to discuss. Client confidentiality."

For which he was eternally thankful. He'd hate to burst his little brother's bubble and ruin his badass image by telling him that he hadn't so much been escorting the "beautiful woman" as the bra she was wearing, and that he'd ultimately lost it. Griff grimaced.

No doubt he'd get his Cool Card revoked for that.

"Ah…" Justin sighed knowingly, as though that element only added another degree of awesomeness to Griff's job. He rather liked this big-brother business, a fact he'd decided to share with his mother and sister as soon as this issue with the bra was settled.

Of course, having that settled unwittingly settled other things—like his relationship with Jess—so there was a part of him that hoped (horrible, he knew) that Payne was wrong about his friend, that Keller wouldn't keep his promise to return it. Because that would keep Jess at his side, looking for it, and they could keep having amazing sex and she could keep scaring the hell out of him with her insightful little peeks into his head.

It was unnerving and yet…not. On one hand, it was nice not having to explain everything, on the other it could be damn inconvenient, particularly when she saw something he didn't want her to see. Like last night, when she'd caught him looking at her and she'd known he'd been thinking about what would happen when they got the bra back.

"We're here *now*," she'd said. "Stop fretting, stop planning and kiss me."

And he had, from one end of her lovely body to the other.

How unfair, he thought, that he'd never met a woman

he could see any sort of future with—and hadn't wanted to—until now, and she lived in another state, too far to drive on a regular basis, and was too firmly entrenched in her life there to relocate.

He didn't have to ask—and wouldn't have anyway—he *knew*.

Because he was in the same position. New job, new life. And even if he could bring himself to leave the job, there was no way in hell he could leave his family again, not after spending years away from them in the military. It would break his mother's heart. Glory would be crushed and disappointed. And then there was Justin, whom he was only just getting to know.

It was an impossible situation, with ultimately no good outcome. He didn't see any way to make the relationship last long term and because of that, logic demanded that they make a clean break when this was done.

The very idea made his brain seize, his chest spasm uncomfortably, made him want to gather her up and haul her to the bedroom and make love to her until they were both covered in sweat, screaming with release, and he'd ruined her for any other man.

A beep sounded over the line, alerting him to another call and he asked Justin to hold on.

It was Payne.

Dread ballooned in his gut.

"Hey, Justin, I've got to take this call. Business," he explained. "I'll check in with you in a day or two, okay?"

"Yeah, sure," he said. "That would be great. And

maybe we could get together," he said, his voice suddenly thinner with nerves. "Go to a ball game or something."

"Sounds good," Griff said, meaning it. He quickly ended the call and accepted the other. "Payne?"

Jess's head swiveled around and she stared at him, wide-eyed and expectant. They both knew that Keller had contacted Payne last night and had set up a meeting today. It had been hours ago, so many, in fact, that Griff had begun to suspect that Keller had been a no-show.

"I've got it," Payne said. "I'll meet you at the office in an hour."

Griff released a slow breath. "All right. We'll see you then."

"Well?" Jess asked. Her voice was neither hopeful nor flat, just cautiously curious.

"He's got it," he said, his gaze tangling with hers. "We're meeting him at the office in an hour."

She swallowed, then offered him a shaky smile. "Dad will be relieved."

"I'm sure he will."

She pushed to her feet, tunneled her fingers through her hair. "I should probably get packed," she said. She started toward the back, then stopped, a question in her gaze. "I've got time for a quick shower, though," she said, a wan smile curling her lips. "Wanna join me?"

More than his next breath, Griff thought. More than anything in this world, or any other.

14

"Wow," GRIFF BREATHED the next morning. "This is *amazing.*"

"Thank you," Jess told him, tucking a strand of hair behind her ear. They'd made half the eight-hour drive yesterday, then spent the night at a quaint little B and B Griff had found online while she'd been packing up—a nice surprise, she had to admit—and had finished the rest of the journey this morning. Her anxiety had increased with each mile they'd covered, and by the time they'd driven past the city limits sign, she'd been a twitchy wreck.

It felt odd having him here in her space. Not wrong, precisely, just different. Probably because she knew it would be the only time he ever visited her house. He would never spend the night with her, wake up in her bed. She'd never cook him breakfast, or cuddle on the couch with him and watch movies when it rained.

A lump welled in her throat and she determinedly swallowed. She'd known this was the inevitable outcome. He had, too. That's why he'd joined her in the shower and taken her so hard and so desperately that they'd brought the shower curtain down and made the menagerie of pets in Payne's apartment above Griff's howl in response to their own screams.

They'd reached the end of this magical romance and despite the fact that it was bittersweet, she wouldn't have missed it for anything. She wouldn't change a single second of any minute she'd spent with him.

It had taken her father less than an hour to make the necessary repairs and, because she hadn't wanted an audience when they ultimately parted ways, she'd asked him to bring her home. She preferred to lick her wounds in private.

"What time are you supposed to meet the Mont-wheeler rep?" she asked.

He swallowed. "Seven. He's got a red-eye flight back to Angola."

Seven. Right. If he didn't leave in the next few minutes, he'd be late, Jess thought, sliding her suddenly shaking palms over the front of her jeans. Oh, Jesus. This was going to be much harder than she'd anticipated.

Evidently her expression betrayed her, because his face was suddenly anguished, his gaze helpless and concerned. He took a step forward. "Jess, I—"

She bit her lip, squeezed her eyes shut and shook her head. "Don't," she said, her voice barely above a whisper. "We both know how this has to p-play out. You're there and I'm here and that's not going to change." She fought back tears and lifted her chin. "We'd only make it work long enough to become more invested, and then we'd be in for double the heartache when it inevitably...didn't." She felt her lips tremble with a sad smile. "You know I'm right," she said, her gaze clinging to his. "I'm not saying anything that hasn't already crossed your mind."

He didn't deny it because he couldn't. She knew him too well.

He shook his head, blew out a breath, seemingly at a loss. "I don't know what to say," he said, lifting his massive shoulders, his gaze tormented.

"Say that you've had a wonderful time, that you've enjoyed my company, that you wish me well and that you'll see me soon."

His gaze sharpened with a question.

"I'll know that it's a lie," she said, hugging her arms to her middle. "But I'd prefer it to goodbye."

Griff finally nodded, lessened the distance between them and hugged her close. She wrapped her arms around his waist, breathed in the scent of him, the feel of him, determined to commit it to memory.

He drew back to look at her, framed her face with his hands and gently stroked her cheeks. His gaze caught and held hers. "I've had a wonderful time," he said. "I've enjoyed your company, I think that you are the most amazing woman I've ever met in my life and knowing you has made me a better man." A sheepish smile tugged at his lips. "I'm ad-libbing at bit," he confided. "It's been an honor and a privilege getting to know you. You've touched my life more than you will ever know. I wish you well, Jessalyn Rossi." He bent and pressed a lingering kiss to her lips, could feel him trembling beneath her hands. Finally—horribly—he drew back. "I'll see you later."

And then he was gone. She watched him walk to the door, heard him descend the steps and listened as the gravel popped beneath his tires as he drove away.

She gasped and her hand flew to her mouth. He'd told her what she meant to him, but she hadn't gotten the chance to tell him what he meant to her. And now it was too late.

She sat carefully on the edge of her sofa, dropped her head into her hands and let the tears fall, quiet sobs racking her body until exhaustion finally claimed her. She awoke the next morning to the sound of a ringing phone and a yowling cat, her face sticky with salt, her eyes puffy and swollen.

She scrambled to the phone and checked the display. Her father. She hadn't expected Griff to call—he'd respect her wishes—but couldn't deny the pinprick of disappointment when it wasn't him.

"Jess, could you come down to the store?" her father asked. "There's something I need to tell you."

She rubbed her eyes, felt her stomach lurch. "Can it wait, Dad? I'm feeling a little queasy this morning." And beat up and gutted and wretched.

"Sorry, sweetheart," he said regretfully. "It can't."

She swallowed a sigh, pushed her hair away from her face. Oh, well, she thought. Back to business as usual.

The world waited for no one, least of all the heart-broken.

THOUGH HE'D NEVER been one to feel sorry for himself, Griff stared at the television, nursed a tumbler of scotch and decided it was about time he tried the sensation out.

He was miserable and he was going to allow himself to be miserable for a little while. Leaving Jess had been the most difficult thing he'd ever done, probably because it had felt so…unnatural. He wasn't supposed to leave her. She wasn't supposed to be away from him. She was supposed to be by his side, under his arm, in his bed. But he'd done what she'd asked because he'd known she was right. But if this was right, then what the hell did *wrong* feel like? What did—

A knock sounded at his first door, cutting him off midtirade. He frowned and set his glass aside. He hadn't expected company. Both his mother and sister were at work, and Justin was attending a college-preview day at the University of Georgia. He fully expected to hear all about it later—and looked forward to it—but there wasn't anyone else he could think of who'd show up unannounced.

Unless it was… His heart jumped into an irregular rhythm. Jess?

He lengthened his stride, reached the door and peered through the peephole.

Shock detonated through him. Not Jess.

Priscilla Wicklow.

Despite everyone's best efforts to stay out of each other's way, he'd seen her at the hospital, hovering at Justin's side. Feeling more than a little off balance, Griff cautiously opened the door. "Priscilla?"

She smiled nervously. She looked thinner than the

last time he'd seen her, Griff noticed. Her hair was clean and styled, but lacking shine. She was quite pale and her skin seemed slack on her bones.

"I know that I'm the last person you ever expected to see on your doorstep, Griff, but I would really appreciate it if you'd allow me to talk to you."

He waited for the old resentment to surface, the anger he'd carried with him since he was thirteen years old, but it didn't come. He nodded. "Come on in," he said, ushering her inside.

She made the tentative walk down his hallway, then waited for him to ask her to sit down before taking a seat.

"Can I get you something to drink?" he asked, still wary of this visit. Honestly, if she was here to lobby on behalf of his father, then she'd better not get too comfortable. That was never going to happen.

She shook her head. "No, thanks."

"What can I do for you?" he asked. Better to get this over with, whatever it turned out to be.

She glanced nervously at him, hesitated. "I've rehearsed this in my head a thousand times over the last six months," she said, looking heavenward. "And now that I'm here and it's time—" she swallowed and lifted a frail shoulder "—I don't know where to start."

While he pitied her, he didn't know where either.

She sucked in a breath, presumably for courage, then turned to face him once more. "I'm dying, Griff," she said.

Out of everything she might have said, that particular revelation had never occurred to him. He was stunned, utterly astounded.

"Pancreatic cancer," she said. "They found it when Justin got sick, when I was tested for a match."

"I'm sorry," he said, still reeling. "Are you certain? Have you consulted a different doctor? Gotten a second opinion?"

Her lips tugged into a sad smile. "And a third and a fourth. It's inoperable and I decided against treatment because I knew I'd need to see Justin through his illness. He doesn't know," she added. Her gaze turned inward and she gave her head a little shake. "I can't think of how to tell him."

He couldn't either and he couldn't begin to imagine the pain his brother was about to go through. Poor kid. He—

"Your father does know. And he's left, again, this time for good, I imagine."

Again? For good? But… Ah, he thought, remembering Jess's remark. *If your father has been such a wonderful dad to him—when historically he's proven that he's not—then why is Justin trying so desperately to have a relationship with you? Is it just because you gave him the kidney? Or is it something else?*

She leaned forward. "I'm not here to make excuses for myself," she said. "But there is something that I want you to know. I didn't know your father was married," she said. "I didn't find out until after he'd left, after I was pregnant. I know that doesn't absolve me of the hurt inflicted upon your family, but I do hope that it makes enough of a difference that you won't hold my mistakes or your father's against my s-son." Her eyes welled with unshed tears. "Because, once I'm gone, he's not going to have anyone. His father might not have divorced me, but he's been gone from our so-called home more than he's been in it. And he's been around for Justin even less." She leaned forward and clasped his hand, the strength in her fingers surprising him. "My boy is going to need you, Griff. You and your sister, if she's willing. Can you be there for him?" she asked, her eyes blazing with hope. "Will you look after him? Please."

It took a minute for Griff to find his voice. "Of course I will," he told her. "He's my brother, isn't he? He'll always have a place with me."

Priscilla wilted with relief, her hand on his going slack and she nodded, tears of gratitude spilling down her cheeks. "Thank you," she said, her voice thick. "You're a good man. A good man," she repeated.

Griff didn't know why finding out his father hadn't been Husband of the Year or Best Dad Ever had surprised him, but it did. He'd always assumed that his father was an integral part of the family he'd abandoned them for, that he wouldn't have left them for anything less.

He couldn't have been more wrong.

He'd simply maintained his true character, that of a lazy, undependable, cheating sack of shit.

And yet, he knew his mother had still cared for him, knew that Priscilla did as well, or she'd have left him.

"Can I ask you something?" Griff queried.

"Of course."

He hesitated, not wanting to be unkind, but... "Why did you stay? If he was so horrible, why did you stay?"

She smiled wearily, almost fatalistically. "I have asked myself that same question over and over again, and I suspect that my answer is the same as your mother's." She shrugged helplessly. "Because I love him," she admitted simply. "I'm not proud of it. I wish that I was stronger, that I'd made better choices. But that's the funny thing about love—*you* don't get to choose, *it* chooses for you. And when the person you love loves you back—even if you know it won't, can't last—there is *nothing* more wonderful in the whole entire world. *Nothing* more powerful."

A tingling started in the balls of his feet and swept upward immediately following her explanation.

You don't get to choose—it chooses for you. And when the person you love loves you back—even if you know it won't, can't last—there is nothing more wonderful in the whole entire world. Nothing more powerful.

He'd been wrong, Griff realized, his insides trembling. More wrong than he'd ever been in his life. So what if he wouldn't get to see her as often as he wanted? So what if they lived in different states? So what if their relationship would be unconventional? This was Jess, after all, he thought wildly, and since when had she ever given a damn about convention?

It was the time they'd get to be together that counted, that was special, and he damn sure wasn't throwing it away on something as mundane as logic.

He shot to his feet, smiled awkwardly. "Priscilla, I don't mean to be rude, but I've got somewhere to go."

"Of course," she said, gathering her purse. He patiently herded her to the door. "Thank you, again, Griff. You can't know what a comfort this is."

He smiled at her, ached for the journey she had ahead of her. "I'm glad I could help. I'll be in touch," he promised.

She leaned up and pressed a kiss against his cheek. "I'd like that very much."

He would, too, he realized as he watched her turn to go. The instant she left, he sprang into action, hurried to his room and started slinging clothes into a bag. He didn't know how long he was going to be gone— however long it took to convince her—so he packed liberally and planned to call Payne from the road. He was between assignments at the moment and if anything came up, then surely another agent could handle it while he got this sorted out.

He'd just buzzed through the apartment, killed all the lights and grabbed his keys when another knock landed against his door.

Bag in hand, he swore violently under his breath and swung it open, prepared to send whoever it was packing.

Jess.

He blinked, staggered.

"Do you have a minute?" she asked uncertainly. Her gaze dropped to his bag and her eyes widened. "Oh, you're leaving. I'm sorry. I—"

"I was coming to see you," he said, his voice ringing strangely in his ears. God, she was lovely, simply breathtaking.

"Coming to see me?" she repeated, looking equally shocked.

"Yes, I was," he said. "I was coming to tell you how wrong we were about us." Remembering himself, he quickly stepped back. "Come in," he said. "Please."

She nodded, and walked past him, her rosy scent trailing along behind her, and he breathed her in, felt his chest constrict with emotion. He dropped his bag, hurried around her and turned on a few of the lights he'd just extinguished.

Rather than sit, she stood in the middle of the room, uncharacteristically nervous, her eyes haunted with wariness. "Before you tell me how wrong we were about us, would it be okay if I said a few things to you?"

"You can say whatever you want to me, Jess."

She smiled a little and fidgeted. "The other day when you left my house, I realized that it was before I got to tell you what you mean to me, how you've made me a better woman."

He shook his head. Bullshit. She was phenomenal long before she'd ever met him. "I—"

She scowled, chastising him. "You said I could do this, remember?"

"I did," he admitted. "Sorry, go on."

"I didn't get to tell you that I had the most wonderful time of my life with you, that you make me feel like I can leap tall buildings in a single bound, or swing through the jungle from one vine to another, or any of the other things that superheroes do."

He grinned. Only Jess. "You mean like superhero guys do?"

She bit the corner of her lip, her eyes twinkling. "Yes, like superhero *guys,* but kick-ass superhero girls aren't nearly as prevalent or as awesome."

"What about Gladiator Girl?"

She snorted indelicately. "What about her? All she's got is a Trident of Truth and she's powerless if a man touches her." She rolled her eyes. "Sorry, but I'd rather *fly.*"

Of course she would. He chuckled, unable to help himself.

"Anyway, I didn't come here to debate the merit of superhero men versus superhero women," she continued impatiently. "I'm here because I needed you to know how special you are to me and how much I enjoyed being with you and how fabulous I think you are." She smiled softly, admiration lighting her gaze. "You're more than just criminally, unfairly handsome," she said, "you're a *genuinely good guy.* You're a rare breed, Griffin Wicklow, and I...I just needed you to know that."

He swallowed thickly, touched, and nodded. "Thank you."

She clasped her hands behind her back and rocked on her heels. "Now it's your turn," she said.

He frowned. "My turn?"

"To tell me why we were wrong about us."

Oh, right. He'd been so overcome with her little speech, he'd momentarily forgotten himself again.

Was that part of being in love? he wondered. Early-onset dementia?

Because he was in love with her. Totally, completely, unequivocally.

He looked up at her, his gaze moving over the dear line of her face. The achingly familiar slope of her cheek, the smooth brow, those unusual gray eyes, her lush mouth. "We were wrong about us...because I love you."

She stilled.

He lifted a single shoulder. "There are more reasons, but ultimately that's what it boils down to." He swallowed and lifted his chin. "I'm in love with you and I'd rather spend whatever time I can with you than none at all. I don't care where you live, or where I live, or how difficult it's going to be. It only matters that I get to see you again." He managed a grin, and peered at her, trying to gauge her expression. "I'm your 'slathering hound,' remember? And I'm not opposed to begging at your back door."

At long last a slow smile slid across her lips and lit her crinkling gaze. "You don't have to beg, Griff."

Relief wilting through him, he sidled forward and wrapped his arms around her. She hugged him back, then tilted her head and pressed a kiss against his neck. "I'm in love with you, too," she whispered. "Crazily so."

"Then we can be insane together."

She smiled up at him. "And guess what?"

"What?"

"As it happens, I'm going to be relocating to Atlanta."

He felt his eyes widen, happiness darting through him, and he gave his head a little shake. "What? Really? When?"

"Really," she said. "My dad met someone online, a woman who lives in an upscale retirement complex here in Atlanta. Twilight Acres," she said. "Anyway, the reason he was so desperate to make sure the business was well on its feet was so that he could leave it to me without worrying about it failing. He's moving here, to be with her."

"What about his agoraphobia?" Griff asked, still reeling from surprise.

"She's arranged for a therapist and he says that he wants to get help, that if it brings them together then it's worth it."

He hummed under his breath. "Sounds like a smart man. But what about your house? The shop?"

"I'm renting the house to Monica at a very affordable rate," she said, her eyes dancing. "Her kids will *love* it."

He grinned. "Understandably."

"And I'm putting the shop up for sale and taking the whole business digital. We already do a huge online business." She shrugged. "It's merely a matter of adding the rest."

"It sounds like you've got everything worked out."

She winced and bit her lip. "Everything but a place to stay," she said, peeking at him through lowered lashes. "I'll need to start looking—"

"No, you don't," he said. "Your place is here with me."

She smiled hesitantly. "Are you sure? That's a pretty big step. I'd understand if you'd rather I—"

"Jess, I've never been more certain of anything in my life. It's go-big-or-go-home time. I want *this* to be your home. *Our* home. At least for the time being, until we can find a nice little plot of land and build our own tree house."

He brushed his lips over hers and she felt that kiss all the way to the bottom of her feet. The wedding march cued up in her head again and a vision of little chubby-cheeked babies with coppery curls suddenly filled her head, making her ovaries scream.

"What do you say?" he asked, his gaze searching hers.

Jess grinned. "Sounds like a plan to me."

His best one yet, she thought, then kissed him again.

Epilogue

One week later...

JESS DIDN'T KNOW why Payne had insisted that she be a part of this Ranger Security meeting, but assumed it was because it had something to do with the Owl—aka Keller Thompson—and her newly engaged status to Griff. She inwardly preened and gazed at the ring on her finger, a simple diamond, set in platinum. It was perfect, just like her fiancé.

"I appreciate all of you coming in this evening," Payne said. "The truth is, I have a huge favor to ask and it's going to take everyone's cooperation to make it work. If any one of you object, then that'll be the end of it, and the issue will never be brought forward again."

Looking as intrigued as concerned, every eye in the boardroom rested on the head of Ranger Security and waited for him to continue.

"As you all know, Keller is an old friend and, despite his...history, he's one I still trust and still value. When all this started with the Clandestine bra, I told

Griff at the time that Keller didn't do anything without a reason, without thinking several steps ahead to an endgame." He paused, then released an imperceptible breath, revealing the first bit of nervousness. "That endgame was a job with Ranger Security."

Silence thundered for all three seconds, then Griff, Flanagan and McCann all swore and offered several creative variations of "Hell, no."

"I understand and anticipated this initial reaction," Payne continued. "But I do wish you'd take a few minutes and think about it before giving me your answer."

"Why didn't he just call you and apply for a job, like a normal person?" Flanagan wanted to know. "Why go to all the trouble to steal something just to give it back? It's illogical."

"Because he was hired by Montwheeler, as well," Griff remarked knowingly, startling the hell out of everyone except Payne, who merely grinned at him.

"What? No way," McCann scoffed.

"He's right," Payne confirmed. "They wanted the additional publicity, wanted to create more buzz, wanted to generate more interest for their company and for the auction."

Flanagan shook his head, passed a hand over his face, then nodded. "And considering that the bra went for a cool million more than it was worth—"

"Because it had been taken from the notorious Owl," McCann interjected, his eyes widening with shock.

"—their plan definitely worked," Flanagan finished. He swore, blinked. "Wow. Just wow."

"Be that as it may, Payne...he's still a thief," Mc-

Cann pointed out. "What sort of message does that send to our clients?"

"He's a *former* thief," Payne corrected. "I think he'd be an invaluable asset to our team. Who better to catch a thief than another thief?" he asked. "Consider this latest case that just landed on my desk. The missing guitar? Keller knows the ins and outs of this market, he knows every reputable fence and, more important, he has the sources to get information that we can't."

"Maybe so," Flanagan said with a shrug. "But I still think that it's risky."

Jess gave her head a shake. "So in addition to getting paid for it, stealing the bra was ultimately his way of interviewing for a job with you? Of proving his merit? The benefit he'd bring to the company?"

Payne nodded. "That was it exactly," he confirmed. "And, much as it pains me to admit, he bested us. I think we're stronger with him and I believe in second chances."

Griff finally looked up. "And what happens if he ends up being a liability? If he ends up stealing from a client, rather than protecting what needs to be protected?"

"If I genuinely thought that would happen, then I wouldn't have brought it to the table," Payne said. "But if it does, then it's on me and I'll make whatever restitution is required."

McCann studied his friend for a long, tense moment. "I trust your judgment," he finally said. "You've never steered this company wrong, and I've got money in the bank and a full belly because of it. If you're willing to take the risk on Keller, then you have my support."

Payne nodded, seemingly touched. "Thank you."

"Mine, as well," Flanagan said. "Guy is right. There wouldn't have been a Ranger Security without you." He managed a smile. "It's easy to forget stuff like that when you're working with your best friends, but it's the truth."

Griff shifted, rubbed the back of his neck. "I'm not at all certain why you thought you needed my vote," he said. "I'm low man on the totem pole here and, frankly, I don't think I deserve a say one way or the other."

"First of all, there are no low men on the totem pole at Ranger Security," Payne told him. "And while it's true that me, Jamie and Guy are partners, it was your mission that Keller thwarted. I wouldn't dream of bringing him on board without discussing it with you and Jess first."

"Thank you," Griff said, obviously grateful. "I appreciate that. And it's for that reason that I'll withhold any objection to Keller joining our team."

Payne's gaze swung to Jess. "And you, Jess? Are you okay with it?"

She chuckled and shook her head. "Who am I to say no? Because of him, business is booming. All's well that ends well, right?"

Payne's cool face melted into a pleased smile and he nodded. "All right then. I'll bring him in."

"What? Now?" Jamie asked in surprise.

"He's here?" McCann echoed, his eyes wide.

"He is," Payne said. "I thought it best to strike while the iron was hot."

Less than a minute later the newest member of Ranger Security and the notorious thief called the Owl followed Payne into the room. Jess didn't know what she'd expected—maybe that he'd look a little more bird-like—but Keller Thompson was definitely a surprise.

He was tall and nice-looking, with dark blond wavy hair and pale green eyes. He had an easy smile, which revealed a set of dimples on either side of his mouth, and moved with a laconic sort of grace. It took him less than two minutes to charm away any reservations the other men might have had about him, and when he finally stepped forward to shake her hand, there was an odd twinkle in his eye, one that she felt she should recognize but didn't.

"Nice to officially meet you, Jess," he said. "I'm a big admirer of your work."

"Yours was pretty impressive, as well," she said.

"I dabble," he said demurely. "Nothing more."

"I'd planned on cleaning your clock," Griff told him. "Because you scared her half to death when you gassed us. But now that you're officially a coworker, I'll refrain."

"Thank you." He winced, leaned in closer to Jess. "My apologies for that," he added. "I'd underestimated his importance to you or I would have used an alternate method, one that wouldn't have been so upsetting."

Her gaze slid to Griff, who'd wandered over to speak to Payne. "Until that moment I'd underestimated his importance to me as well, so you're forgiven."

"And business is well?" he asked.

She grinned. "Very well." As she was sure he knew. Her cell suddenly vibrated in her pocket and she winced and excused herself. "Sorry," she said. "It's probably my dad."

Jess turned away and glanced at the phone, surprised when she realized it hadn't rung, but that she'd gotten a text. A picture.

It was the selfie Andre had taken with his cell phone the day of the show. He was leaned over her shoulder, smiling widely, his hand dangling over her other shoulder, and in that hand…was the owl feather that she'd later found on Payne's chest.

She gasped, stunned, and whirled around, looking for Keller. It was impossible, she thought. Different hair, different eyes, different voice. What about the dog? What about his boyfriend?

Holy mother of…

He'd staged it all. Every damn bit of it.

Finally, her gaze caught his and he winked at her.

Her phone suddenly hooted twice and then the image vanished from her screen, the only verifiable evidence that Keller Thompson had been Andre the stylist.

Another text arrived. It'll be our little secret, eh?

Griff sidled up next to her. "Are you all right?" he asked, concern lighting his gaze. "You look odd."

She gave herself a little shake. "I'm fine," she said. "I seem to have lost my dog," she pretended to fret. "Have you seen him?"

Griff chuckled and slung an arm around her shoulders. "Attach the leash, baby, and let's go home."

She sighed and lifted her lips up for a kiss. "Another plan I can fully get behind."

"You know me," he teased. "The man with the plan."

* * * * *

COMING NEXT MONTH FROM

HARLEQUIN®

Blaze®

Available September 17, 2013

#767 LYING IN YOUR ARMS
Forbidden Fantasies • by Leslie Kelly

Madison Reid's engagement to a Hollywood superstar made her the envy of every woman. Only, the engagement was a sham and now, it's pretty well over. Still, she has her work cut out for her in convincing firefighter Leo Santori—her hot holiday fling—of that fact....

#768 THE MIGHTY QUINNS: ROURKE
The Mighty Quinns • by Kate Hoffmann

Annie Macintosh has lived her whole life as an outcast, scarred by childhood tragedy. But her solitary existence is turned upside down with the arrival of Rourke Quinn and a nor'easter that threatens to change her world in more ways than one.

#769 THE BRIDESMAID'S BEST MAN
by Susanna Carr

Bridesmaid Angie Lawson is stunned when her ex, Cole Foster, turns up unexpectedly, insisting that he's undercover and needs her help. Angie's tempted, especially given her memories of how *good* he was *under* the covers....

#770 COMMAND PERFORMANCE
Uniformly Hot! • by Sara Jane Stone

Maggie Barlow, a professor writing a behind-the-scenes book about the Army Rangers, discovers her one-night stand—the man she asked to fulfill *all* her fantasies—holds the key to her success.

**YOU CAN FIND MORE INFORMATION ON UPCOMING HARLEQUIN® TITLES,
FREE EXCERPTS AND MORE AT WWW.HARLEQUIN.COM.**

HBCNM0913

REQUEST YOUR FREE BOOKS!
2 FREE NOVELS PLUS 2 FREE GIFTS!

HARLEQUIN®

Blaze®

red-hot reads!

YES! Please send me 2 FREE Harlequin® Blaze™ novels and my 2 FREE gifts (gifts are worth about $10). After receiving them, if I don't wish to receive any more books, I can return the shipping statement marked "cancel." If I don't cancel, I will receive 4 brand-new novels every month and be billed just $4.74 per book in the U.S. or $4.96 per book in Canada. That's a savings of at least 14% off the cover price. It's quite a bargain. Shipping and handling is just 50¢ per book in the U.S. and 75¢ per book in Canada.* I understand that accepting the 2 free books and gifts places me under no obligation to buy anything. I can always return a shipment and cancel at any time. Even if I never buy another book, the two free books and gifts are mine to keep forever.

150/350 HDN F4WC

Name   (PLEASE PRINT)

Address   Apt. #

City   State/Prov.   Zip/Postal Code

Signature (if under 18, a parent or guardian must sign)

Mail to the **Harlequin® Reader Service:**
IN U.S.A.: P.O. Box 1867, Buffalo, NY 14240-1867
IN CANADA: P.O. Box 609, Fort Erie, Ontario L2A 5X3

Want to try two free books from another line?
Call 1-800-873-8635 or visit www.ReaderService.com.

* Terms and prices subject to change without notice. Prices do not include applicable taxes. Sales tax applicable in N.Y. Canadian residents will be charged applicable taxes. Offer not valid in Quebec. This offer is limited to one order per household. Not valid for current subscribers to Harlequin Blaze books. All orders subject to credit approval. Credit or debit balances in a customer's account(s) may be offset by any other outstanding balance owed by or to the customer. Please allow 4 to 6 weeks for delivery. Offer available while quantities last.

Your Privacy—The Harlequin® Reader Service is committed to protecting your privacy. Our Privacy Policy is available online at www.ReaderService.com or upon request from the Harlequin Reader Service.

We make a portion of our mailing list available to reputable third parties that offer products we believe may interest you. If you prefer that we not exchange your name with third parties, or if you wish to clarify or modify your communication preferences, please visit us at www.ReaderService.com/consumerschoice or write to us at Harlequin Reader Service Preference Service, P.O. Box 9062, Buffalo, NY 14269. Include your complete name and address.

HB13R2

SPECIAL EXCERPT FROM

HARLEQUIN *Blaze*

Bestselling author Leslie Kelly is back
with *another* sizzling Forbidden Fantasy!

Lying in Your Arms

Available September 17, 2013,
wherever Harlequin books are sold.

Leo checked out the rest of the room, pausing in the bathroom to strip out of his clothes and grab a towel, which he
slung over one shoulder. He returned to the patio door, put
one hand on the jamb and another on the slider, and stood
naked in the opening, letting that tropical breeze bathe his
body in coolness.

Heaven.

He was just about to step outside and let the warm late-day
sun soak into his skin when he heard something very out of
place. A voice. A woman's voice. Coming from right behind
him…inside his room.

"Oh. My. God!"

Shocked, he swung around, instinctively yanking the towel
off his shoulder.

A woman stood in his room, staring at him, wide-eyed. They
stared at each other, silent, surprised, and Leo immediately
noticed several things about her.

She was young—his age, maybe. Definitely not thirty.

She was uncomfortable, tired or not feeling well. Her
blouse clung to her curvy body, as it was moist with sweat.

HBEXP79771

Dark smudges cupped her red-rimmed eyes, and she'd already kicked off her shoes, which rested on the floor right by the door, as if her first desire was to get barefoot, pronto.

Oh. And she was hot. Jesus, was she ever.

She was one more thing, he suddenly realized.

Shocked. Stunned. Maybe a little afraid.

"Hi," he said with a small smile. He remained where he was, not wanting to startle her.

Her green eyes moved as she shifted her attention over his body, from bare shoulders, down his chest, then toward the white towel that he clutched in his fist right at his belly. Finally, something like comprehension washed over her face.

"Look, I don't know who put you up to this, but I don't need you."

"Don't need me for what?" *To do your taxes? Cut your hair? Carry your suitcase?*

Put out your fire?

Oh, he suspected he could do that last one, and it wasn't just because of his job.

"To have sex with me."

His jaw fell open. *"What?"*

She licked her lips. "I mean, you're very attractive and all." Her gaze dropped again. "Still, I think you'd better get out."

"I can't do that," he said, his voice low, thick.

He edged closer, unable to resist lifting a hand to brush a long, drooping curl back from her face, tucking it behind her ear.

"Why not?" she whispered.

"Because you're in my room."

**Pick up LYING IN YOUR ARMS by Leslie Kelly,
on sale September 17, 2013,
wherever Harlequin® Blaze® books are sold.**

Copyright © 2013 by Leslie A. Kelly

HBEXP79771

Every bachelorette party has a surprise...

And for Angie Lawson it's seeing her ex-boyfriend at a strip club, standing right in front of her—every sexy, delicious inch of him. Cole Foster isn't the kind of guy that *any* woman can just ignore....

Cole's working undercover and needs Angie's help to get into the bridal party. And if getting there means getting her in bed, too, then he's *definitely* the best man for the job!

Pick up

The Bridesmaid's Best Man

by *Susanna Carr,*

available September 17, 2013, wherever you buy Harlequin Blaze books.

HARLEQUIN®

Blaze®

Red-Hot Reads
www.Harlequin.com

HB79773

Mission: Keep Margaret Barlow distracted...using any means necessary!

All professor Maggie Barlow wanted was a night of wicked satisfaction from the dead-sexy ranger, Hunter Cross. Having him as her official army liaison while she works on her new book? That *wasn't* in the plan. Especially when she learns that Hunter has orders to "control" her. Little does the army know that when it comes to their deliciously naughty nighttime activities, Hunter is at Maggie's complete command....

Pick up

Command Performance

by *Sara Jane Stone,*
available September 17, 2013, wherever you buy Harlequin Blaze books.

⊕HARLEQUIN®

Blaze®

Red-Hot Reads
www.Harlequin.com

HB79774

HARLEQUIN®
A *Romance* FOR EVERY MOOD™

Love the Harlequin book you just read?

Your opinion matters.

Review this book on your favorite book site, review site, blog or your own social media properties and share your opinion with other readers!

Be sure to connect with us at:
Harlequin.com/Newsletters
Facebook.com/HarlequinBooks
Twitter.com/HarlequinBooks

HREVIEWS

HARLEQUIN®

A *Romance* FOR EVERY MOOD™

Stay up-to-date on all your romance-reading news with the *Harlequin Shopping Guide,* featuring bestselling authors, exciting new miniseries, books to watch and more!

The newest issue will be delivered right to you with our compliments! There are 4 each year.

Signing up is easy.

EMAIL

ShoppingGuide@Harlequin.ca

WRITE TO US

HARLEQUIN BOOKS
Attention: Customer Service Department
P.O. Box 9057, Buffalo, NY 14269-9057

OR PHONE

1-800-873-8635 in the United States
1-888-343-9777 in Canada

Please allow 4-6 weeks for delivery of the first issue by mail.